Tinyburg Revisited

Tinyburg Revisited

ROBERT J. HASTINGS

BROADMAN PRESS
Nashville, Tennessee

4257-35
ISBN: 0-8054-5735-6

Dewey Decimal Classification: SC
Subject heading: SHORT STORIES // CHRISTIAN LIFE—FICTION

Library of Congress Catalog Card Number: 88-6968
Printed in the United States of America

The story "A Ride Around the Block" first appeared in *Mature Living* magazine, Apr. 1987, pp. 34*ff.* © Copyright 1987, The Sunday School Board of the Southern Baptist Convention. Used by permission. The story "The Quilt" first appeared in *Home Life* magazine, Mar. 1986, pp. 34*ff.* © Copyright 1987, The Sunday School Board of the Southern Baptist Convention. Used by permission. "The Station" which is quoted in the story "The Tinyburg Station" is used by permission of Robert J. Hastings.

Library of Congress Cataloging-in-Publication Data

Hastings, Robert J.
   Tinyburg revisited / Robert J. Hastings.
      p.   cm.
   ISBN 0-8054-5735-6 :
   1. Short stories.   I. Title.
BV4832.2.H3344   1988
813'.54—dc19   88-6968
                                                                          CIP

Dedicated to

Jay Greener, Producer,
"Tinyburg Tales" broadcasts
Radio WBGL, Champaign, IL

Foreword

In the Athabascan Indian dialect, *chuysh wantec* meant "chop off half the winter." Thus, a pleasing compliment to an Indian storyteller was *"Chuysh wantec!"* meaning "You make a short winter!"

A good story informs, entertains, and inspires. It also makes the time pass quickly. How often has a 45-minute message seemed like 15 minutes, because the speaker made good use of story and illustration.

Tinyburg Revisited is a collection of stories based on everyday life in that mythical village of Tinyburg, population 1,473. This small town is easy to find, since it's exactly seven miles south of Pretense. And at the edge of town is this huge billboard: "Welcome to Tinyburg, the only city in the United States with an unlisted zip code!"

Although the characters are fictional, we often see ourselves in them—Candice Spiller depressed over her fortieth birthday, or Ed Ramsey spading up a flower bed for his wife, Pearl, at their new home in Tinyburg, so she won't miss the farm from which they retired.

Abraham Lincoln confessed that a good story was like a medicine to his bones.

Storytelling is thousands of years old. Prehistoric drawings on the walls of caves probably depict stories of personal exploits, such as hunting and fishing.

Our English word *story* comes from the Latin word, *historia,* meaning "a picture." Since history consists of anything that has happened that's worth writing down, stories then become word pictures of such events.

Jesus gained the ear of ordinary people not only because He

used simple words but also because He told stories from the everyday lives of his listeners. "And the common people heard him gladly" (Mark 12:37) is one of the finest compliments ever paid to our Lord.

In 1983, Broadman Press published the first collection of my stories, *Tinyburg Tales*. Now, five years later, comes *Tinyburg Revisited*. Whether this is your first trip to Tinyburg—or a return visit—I hope it's a good one.

ROBERT J. HASTINGS

Tinyburg Revisited is fiction, and any resemblance to actual persons, living or dead, is purely coincidental.

Contents

A Ride Around the Block

One of the fascinating residents in Tinyburg is a wheelchair patient, Myrtle Eagleton, age seventy-two. However, I shouldn't describe Myrtle as a patient, as that would insult her.

After an accident paralyzed her left leg four years ago, Dr. G. S. Gordon, the town physican, gave her sound advice:

"Myrtle, there's not a thing we can do about that leg. But the rest of you's fine. You're strong as ever in your arms and shoulders. So don't sit back in a rocking chair and pity yourself. Find some new hobbies. Get out as often as you can. Be sensible, of course, but never give up!"

Myrtle, who lives at 714 Glendale Street, took Dr. Gordon's advice. Naturally, she couldn't jog around the block. But she was determined to keep fit, even in a wheelchair.

She always liked to garden, but now she took new interest in her vegetables and flowers. First, she hired a handyman to rearrange her garden into beds. One bed was for lettuce, radishes, and onions. Another for English peas, beets, and carrots. Another for tomatoes, and so on. Finally, a flower bed for zinnias, marigolds, and petunias.

With grassy strips between the beds, she can maneuver around to do the hoeing, raking, and weeding. To reach the plants from her wheelchair, Myrtle asked Carl W. Bradley, a neighbor, to put extensions on the handles of her lightweight rake and hoe. Carl, a skilled woodcarver, also rigged a pair of clippers to the end of a long pole for her to trim around her flowers and plants.

Mark, a high school boy, usually spades the beds and sets out her plants each spring. But she does the cultivating from her wheelchair.

The sunshine and fresh air was like a tonic, for soon she was sleeping and eating better. Too, she was amazed how the hoeing and raking strengthened her arms.

Gardening did her so much good that she devised a plan to get outdoors the year-round. Here's how. At precisely 9 AM each morning, she wheels herself down a wooden ramp to the sidewalk, then circles the block three times.

She does this regardless of the weather, 365 days a year. An ingenuous person, she made herself a cloak of heavy plastic for rainy and snowy days. Underneath, she wears heavy coats and sweaters as needed. The cloak fits snugly around her neck, big enough to cover her and the wheelchair, but not too long to get tangled in the spokes. A yellow, rubber raincap with a wide brim that turns down in the back completes her bad-weather gear.

If the weather's nice and she doesn't stop to talk, she circles her block in exactly 12 minutes and 20 seconds. This means about 40 minutes for the three round trips.

Hardly a morning passes that Myrtle isn't discussed in at least one of the nine houses in her block, bounded by Glendale, Monroe, Clark, and Logan Streets. "Just saw Myrtle go by . . . must be her third time around . . . you're wrong, it's her second trip . . . thought this rain might keep her inside."

Aunt Sarah Biggs scolded Myrtle one icy morning when she inched past her house on a slick coating of ice and packed snow.

"Myrtle Eagleton, one of these days you're gonna fall on your face and cripple that other leg. No sensible woman would venture out on a morning like this—especially in a wheelchair."

"Thank you, Aunt Sarah," she replied. "But I'd rather leave this world with a broken neck than shrivel up and blow away in a hospital bed. This wheelchair's no one-way ticket to the cemetery for me."

Passing the same nine houses three times a day, month after month, one gets well acquainted. So Myrtle knows and is known by each of the 23 persons who live in those nine houses. She remembers the number of bicycles on the block, the license numbers of the cars in the driveways, and how many doors and windows face the street. Even the cats and dogs know Myrtle Eagleton.

Through the years, these 23 neighbors have become, to her, a big extended family. She's always doing some little favor, but in a special way on birthdays.

On each birthday, she bakes a small, personal cake. "With my other work, I couldn't make a family cake for each birthday," she admits. "But I can manage 23 small ones."

She uses a miniature baking pan, about four by six inches. One popular recipe is for a white cake flavored with lemon. She also bakes chocolate, apple sauce, upside down, carrot, pound, yellow, and angel cakes. Each is the same size and each, in its way, is as tasty a cake as you'd ever want to eat. Extracts fill one shelf of her small kitchen cabinet, and she's constantly thumbing through magazines, looking for new recipes.

Each little cake is a work of art, decorated with a theme all its own. A few weeks before a neighbor's birthday, she inquires as to his or her wish. Since youngsters usually ask for toys, she molds the frosting into a replica of what they want. She's frosted cakes with miniature bicycles, sleeping bags, wagons, dolls, and even an Indian head-dress.

When Aunt Sarah dreamed of a bus trip out West for her fifty-fourth birthday, Myrtle outlined seven Western states on the frosting, in contrasting colors. She then topped the cake with a toy bus.

However, Myrtle insists on baking a "big" cake for each of her 23 neighbors whenever his age is divisible by five, such as 25 or 55. And it's always a four-layer banana cake, her specialty. A neighbor with a birthday divisible by five never lets Myrtle forget. Neither would you, once you sampled her banana cake!

She blends dead-ripe bananas into the batter, as well as slicing firm bananas between each layer. Bananas for the batter must be ripe enough to have brown spots, but not mushy. The bananas sliced between layers must be fully yellow, but firm. Woe to the grocery clerk who can't supply both degrees of ripeness!

Using a warm, caramel frosting made with her secret recipe, she alternates the layers of cake, sliced bananas, and frosting. The warmth of the frosting seals in the banana flavor so pungently that you get hungry thinking about it.

Whenever she delivers a cake to a neighbor, she takes her instamatic camera to make a photo. Her scrapbook is running over with color prints of happy children and adults showing off their cakes.

Oh, I forgot to mention another example of how methodical Myrtle is.

Precisely at 7:30 each morning, she raises the shade of a big picture window in her living room that faces the east. Her houseplants set in front of that window, basking in the sunlight.

The Osborn kids, who live across the street, make a game of watching for Myrtle to raise her shade. "Myrtle's up!" they cry. "Time to catch the school bus."

So now you get the picture of "mythodical" Myrtle—raising her front shade at 7:30, leaving for her morning excursions at 9:00. Never a minute sooner, never a minute later. And if it's someone's birthday, a fresh cake resting on her lap.

But there came the morning when deep depression held Myrtle in bed, like a prison. Her front shade remained closed. Her all-weather cape hung silently in the closet. Her wheelchair sat motionless in a corner.

It all started the day before when she enjoyed a luncheon at the country club in Bigtown. It was the fifty-fifth reunion of her high school class. Only seven ladies and two men attended. The class was small to begin with, and now only a handful remained. The program consisted of a slide presentation by a woman Myrtle hadn't seen in years. She told about her recent trip around the world, illustrating it with color slides.

"One can't imagine the exciting world out there," she began. "Travel gives you a new vista, opens doors to new cultures. Until I made this cruise, I never realized how small was my world. You know what I mean—provincial, inbred, even tacky. I encourage each of you to save for one overseas trip. I saved a lot just by cutting back on Christmas cards, birthday gifts, and wedding showers. I decided it was time to do something for myself."

The color slides were fascinating and Myrtle enjoyed every minute. But when she returned to her four-room house at 714 Glendale, it looked so tiny and drab. Even if she tried, she could never save enough for a world cruise. And where had she been? Around the same block, past 9 houses, meeting 23 people, day after day, hundreds of times. Always taking someone a cake, snapping their photos, concerned over what *they* want!

And what did she have to show for it? A rickety wheelchair she couldn't afford to replace, plus a scrapbook of friends on Glendale, Clark, Monroe, and Logan streets! Not one photo of the Taj Mahal, Buckingham Palace, Niagara Falls, the White House, the Swiss Alps, Christ of the Andes, or the Pyramids.

That's why, at 8:30 the next morning, she was still in bed when an officer of the Tinyburg Police Department knocked.

"Come in," she said weakly, not bothering to raise her voice.

"Just checking, Myrtle," the officer replied as he stuck his head in the door. "Frances, who lives across the street, called us from her job at the courthouse. Seems the school notified her that her kids were absent. When she called home, they said they were waiting for you to raise your shade at 7:30. Said that's their signal to catch the school bus. Frances feared you were ill. Anything I can do?"

"Guess I stayed up too late and overslept," she alibied.

At 9:05 the telephone rang. "That you, Myrtle? You've never been late. Always watch for you. Sort of makes my day. If I'm draggy myself, helps me put on a smile and do something useful."

At 9:10 it rang again. Another neighbor. "Are you okay, Myrtle? Had me worried when I looked out and didn't see you. Figured maybe the world had stopped turning. Wouldn't bother me much if it came to a dead stop. But I never want to see you stop coming 'round our block."

Within 15 minutes, Myrtle got nine calls. Every family on the block missed her.

After the last call, Myrtle began talking to herself. "Folks fly half-way 'round the world to see the Taj Mahal that some ruler built to honor his wife. But here in Tinyburg, I need go only half-way around one block to meet friendly folk, waiting to see me. Guess that's better than all the touristy slide shows in Bigtown!"

With that she slid out of bed into her trusty wheelchair. It was the eightieth birthday of Carl W. Bradley, the widower wood-carver, and not a banana in the house!

She quickly dialed the Tinyburg Market and ordered "five real ripe bananas with brown spots, but not mushy or black" and "seven more ripe bananas, yellow and firm, but no brown spots."

"You're mightly particular," the clerk joked. "You bet I am," Myrtle laughed. "I'm a particular person; this is a particular day; I want particular bananas; and I want them now!"

The middle of the afternoon, Myrtle wheeled herself over to Carl's, his freshly baked cake still warm to her touch.

When Carl opened the door, two big tears coursed down his weathered cheeks. "Oh, honey," he said, "I thought you'd forgotten. I've outlived so many of my family. This is the first birthday I can remember when no one even bought me a card."

Then with trembling hands, he reached out for the four-layer banana cake, warm also in his hands, the rich aroma teasing his taste buds.

Early the next morning, a half hour before time to raise her front shade, Myrtle heard a knock at the door. *Surely not another policeman,* she said to herself. But no, it was Carl.

"Excuse me for coming so early," Carl began. "But I brought you something. A wall plaque for your home. I set up late making it. Then I wrote a little poem and engraved on it."

"You needn't have made a special trip," Myrtle replied. "I'd have been by in a little while. Oh, I know. Since I missed yesterday, you figured I wouldn't be back. Carl, as long as God gives strength in these bony hands to grab ahold of these two wheels, I'll pass your house every morning about 9:07, sink or swim. No one can deny me the joy of seeing the eighth wonder of this old world—wonderful friends like you!"

Now it was Myrtle's turn to wipe her eyes, as she read the plaque. Carl's "poem" would never win a Pulitzer, but it sprang from his heart:

> Before you came,
> My day was night.
> But since you did,
> My night is day.

The plaque now hangs by Myrtle's bed, where she sees it each morning. And if it's cold outside, or raining, or ice on the sidewalks, and she's tempted to pull up the covers and sleep in, the verse nudges her to slip into her wheelchair, raise the front shade, pull on her poncho, and go for three rides around the block!

If you're ever in Tinyburg and need to set your watch, drive up to 714 Glendale any morning before 7:30. Right on the dot,

Myrtle raises her shade and you can adjust your watch. But not a minute later—even 7:31—or you'll miss the show.

Myrtle's Banana Layer Cake

1²/₃ cups sugar
²/₃ cup margarine

2½ cups flour
1¼ teaspoon baking powder
1½ teaspoon baking soda
1 teaspoon salt

⅓ cup buttermilk
2 beaten eggs
1¼ cups ripe, mashed bananas

Blend sugar and margarine. Sift together the flour, baking powder, baking soda, and salt. Combine buttermilk, eggs, and bananas. Alternately blend (a little at a time) the dry ingredients and the moist ingredients with the sugar-margarine. Then beat the whole until fluffy. Pour into three or more (depending on size of your pans) greased and floured round pans. Bake for 30 minutes at 375°.

While cakes are baking, prepare the caramel frosting:

2 cups light brown sugar
2 sticks of butter
²/₃ cup milk
4 cups confection sugar

Combine brown sugar, butter, and milk. Boil for two minutes. Set aside and let cool for 30 minutes. Beat in confection sugar.

Begin frosting the cakes while they are warm. Frost the first layer, then top it completely with sliced circles of fully ripe but firm bananas.

Place second layer on top and repeat process. Do same with the third layer.

When all layers are in place, spread generous amount of frosting over entire cake, including the sides. This may or may not be enough frosting, depending on number of layers and how much you want to use. Myrtle likes a thick frosting! If you have a better recipe, let Myrtle know. She's never too old to learn.

If so, write her at 714 Glendale in Tinyburg. The zip code? Sorry, it's unlisted and I promised never to tell!

"I Remember Dad"

The most memorable Father's Day at the Tinyburg Church was June 19, 1983. The program consisted of testimonies by men over fifty years of age, whose fathers were deceased. Each spoke about seven minutes on the theme, "What I Remember Best About My Dad."

All the speeches were good, but the one folks still talk about was by Earl Baggett. It was so outstanding that the Rotary Club asked him to repeat it at one of their June meetings the following summer.

Earl, who grew up in the thirties on a farm near Tinyburg, described how his Dad could fix nearly anything with baling wire. At first, listeners thought this was inappropriate for the occasion. But as Earl got into his subject, he fascinated them with his testimony. I think you'd like to hear it, too. So I asked him for a copy. Here, in his words, is what he said:

"Like most youngsters who grew up on a family farm in the thirties, I remember how self-sufficient was our way of life. If we needed anything, we didn't jump in a car and drive to town. If Mom wanted to fry some potatoes for supper, she asked one of us kids to dig up a hill or two in the garden. If Dad cut his thumb while chopping kindling, he tore off a strip of white cotton rag and made himself a bandage.

"What I remember best about Dad was the odds and ends of wire he kept in a shed. We called it baling wire, but actually, it was all kinds and sizes. I never knew him to throw away even the smallest lengths. 'Never know when I might need that,' he'd say.

"Back then we had an old tractor and hay baler. Not nearly as sophisticated as the big farm machinery you see today. It

19

was amazing how Dad could use a piece of baling wire to make minor repairs, good enough to hold until he got to town for a spare part.

"By the time I came along, he had sold his plow horses. But he often told me how he once mended the leather harnesses with pieces of wire. I can believe it, for if my pony bridle ever broke, he could mend it quicker than a flash with a length of wire.

"My sister played endlessly with her toy wagon. On Saturdays, she arranged her dolls in the wagon and played going to town. In winter, she bundled them up in little blankets and quilts. 'If you be good, I'll buy you a sack of candy at the store,' she promised them.

"I remember one Saturday when all of her little dolls were dressed and seated in the wagon, ready to go to 'town.' Just then, the wagon tongue came loose and the cotter pin that held it in place got lost in the grass. Boy, did she bawl. That shopping trip was as real to her as anything. But Dad saved the day, with—you guessed it—a piece of baling wire. Even her dolls seemed to smile with gratitude.

"Once he fixed something, Dad had a favorite expression. I can remember his tone of voice: 'This will have to do, until we can do better.'

"Oh, I could talk a week about Dad's baling wire. One Thanksgiving morning when we had a houseful of company, Mom built a fire in her wood cook stove, way before daylight. She'd just baked three of the fattest pumpkin pies you can imagine and was ready to put a ten-pound goose in the oven when one of the hinges on the oven door broke.

"At first, she said she was ruined. All she could think of was to prop the oven door shut with a kitchen chair. But Dad offered a better solution—a piece of his trusty baling wire! Thanksgiving dinner wasn't a minute late, and the goose never dreamed there was a problem of any kind.

"As a class project in the eighth grade, the boys made wren houses. I built three of them—painted each a different color, red, white, and blue. Dad said that since wrens are so friendly and like to be around people, we should put them close to the house. As we had three big maple trees in the front yard, that's where we decided to hang them.

"I wondered if the wind might blow them down but, as usual, Dad had the answer. He fastened them so securely with the wire that one of the biggest thunderstorms I remember, which came on July 4, never nudged them. And the wrens rode out the storm, safe in their little houses. The reason I remember it was on July 4 is that as I saw their little red, white, and blue houses rocking in the wind, the colors reminded me of the fireworks we were to see that night.

"When I was a boy, Dad drove a beat-up pickup. I say beat-up for that's the literal truth. When it finally stopped running for good, there wasn't enough of it left to haul to the junkyard. When the door handle on the driver's side broke clean off, Dad simply wired the door shut and went on about his business.

"Seems we were always breaking an ax handle, or the handles of our hatchets and hammers. Until he could get to the hardware store to buy a new handle, Dad simply took a piece of wire and fastened the broken pieces together. One fall when we were short of cash and even an ax handle was a luxury we couldn't afford, Dad cut most of our kindling wood with an ax held together with wire.

"Each spring, Mom made a scarecrow from our worn-out clothes. She was so clever that once a scarecrow was stuffed, he looked like a real man. In fact, as a little tyke, I remember the first one I saw. I cried and ran in the house, thinking it was a live monster of some kind.

"Once Mom finished the scarecrow, Dad sunk a post in the garden, to which he wired the scarecrow. We had some strong winds, but that old fellow stood there day after day, flapping his arms at the birds, until we took him down in the fall. Scarecrows in our neighbors' gardens often blew down, but not ours.

"When I started to school, Mom wrapped my lunch in newspaper, or maybe put it in a paper sack. Then the Christmas I was in the third grade, my sister and I found real, metal lunch boxes under the tree. You remember how they looked, gay, colorful pictures on the sides of children flying kites, the wind blowing their hair, or riding on merry-go-rounds, picnicking at the lake.

"Whenever school grew boring, I gazed at my lunch box on the shelf and daydreamed I was on a picnic.

"One afternoon on our way home, the school bully teased me and tried to push me down in a mud puddle. Like little David fighting the giant Goliath, I swung my lunch pail with all my might and struck him on the forehead. It made a gash and brought the blood. He was so angry he grabbed the box from me and threw it against the side of a big tree, breaking the handle. I was heartbroken. But Dad knew the answer. He hollowed out the center of a piece of round wood, slipped it over a piece of wire, and made me a new handle. I didn't have to carry my lunch in a paper sack for even one day.

"My best memory of Dad's baling wire dates from when I was a sophomore in high school. As a member of the Future Farmers of America, I attended a judging contest at the state fairgrounds in Bigtown. There were five of us boys who went. How excited we were, staying in a real hotel and being gone overnight.

"The morning we left I was busy packing my clothes in what we then called a suitcase. It barely held everything, for I must have thought I'd be gone a month. I bore all my weight on it to push it shut. Just then, one of the latches broke and half my things spilled out on the bed.

"It was the only piece of luggage we owned and there wasn't time to borrow or buy another. Dad said not worry, that he could wire it shut. That's when I really got mad. I said I wasn't going to be embarrassed in front of my friends, walking into the hotel carrying a suitcase held together with baling wire. I'd stay home first.

"Then Dad went out to the shed and brought in a roll of black friction tape, the kind electricians use. He first wired the case shut, then covered the wire with tape. Since the suitcase was black to begin with, you hardly noticed it. I could have hugged him with joy!

"On this Father's Day, here in Tinyburg Church, I recall fond memories of the aroma of that goose, baking on Thanksgiving morning. And that new lunch box under the Christmas tree. And my sister's wagon, the wren houses, the scarecrows in the garden, Dad's old pickup, his dilapidated tractor, the mended ax handles.

"But best of all, I remember what he said. I heard it a thousand times: 'This will do until we can do better!'

"Friends, there's lots of hurts in this old world. And in our better moments, we think we can make everything like new. We see ourselves as heroes on white horses. But we can't always do that. A makeshift, patched-up job may be our best, for the time being.

"But don't quit patching. Like Dad, let's do what we can, reassuring each other, 'This will do, until we can do better.'"

With that, Earl sat down. And when he did, there wasn't a dry eye in the church.

To this day, Earl keeps a big strand of baling wire in his garage. It's a souvenir from his dad's farm.

But it's more than baling wire. It's bird houses and lunch pails, toy wagons and scarecrows, old tractors and pony bridles, and ax handles and cook stoves.

Most of all, it's about boys and their dads, love and family, and "making do until you can do better."

A Fire in the Church Parlor

"After long consideration, I'm convinced that what Tinyburg Church needs more than anything is a new parlor."

The speaker was Mrs. Clay Barker. The occasion was a monthly church business session. Mr. Barker, president of Tinyburg Realty Company, reinforced her every word with a nod of his plump, round head.

"During our vacation, I attended an afternoon tea in the new parlor of the Bigtown Church. I can't describe how lovely it was . . . the flowers, the silver service, the rich carpeting, the soft lighting."

Church treasurer Theo Casey raised the question of space and cost.

"Simple," Mrs. Barker replied with the confidence of a newly elected politician. "We've got two classrooms just off the foyer that would make an ideal parlor. We can tear out the partitions and make a lovely room. We can combine the two classes which meet there and put them in the furnace room. Neither class has enough members to justify a room of its own, anyway. As for cost, Clay and I'll give the first $1,000. Money's never been a problem in Tinyburg when folks see the need."

Uncle Billy "Told-You-So" Cutrell, sitting near the back, shuffled to his feet. "Mrs. Barker, if you just need a glass of iced tea, why you can go down to the church kitchen and stir you up some instant in no time."

"Uncle Billy," Mrs. Barker replied in a condescending tone, "you don't drink iced tea at a tea. I'm talking about a tea spelled with a capital *T*. Like when someone's going away, or you entertain a visiting dignitary. And it's *hot* tea. And coffee or maybe a nice fruit punch in the summer. And someone pours from a silver tea service, and you serve mints and nuts and maybe finger sandwiches. And you bring in dainty napkins and doilies and real cream and sugar in cubes—not just the granulated kind."

"Sounds like a lot of botheration to me," Uncle Billy replied, still unconvinced. "Oh, you don't understand!" Mrs. Barker replied. "It's not just what you drink, but the feeling you have of standing there, all dressed in your best, and greeting friends, and just knowing you're at a formal tea. I get shivers up my back just thinking about it."

"Takes more than that to shiver me," Uncle Billy shot back.

But Mrs. Barker was so persistent that members voted for the parlor, fully expecting it would, at the least, help to usher in the kingdom of God!

Once word was out, you can imagine how excited folks got about that parlor, some donating precious heirlooms such as a silver tea service. That summer, Vacation Bible School went begging for teachers, for it seemed everyone had a finger in the parlor pie, one way or another. An interior decorator helped coordinate the colors of the walls, drapes, and carpeting which Uncle Billy estimated to be at least two inches thick. Candelabra, a Duncan Phyfe table, a breakfront to hold the china, and plush couches and settees gave the new parlor a "made-in Bigtown" look. The society editor of *Bigtown News*, who attended the ribbon cutting, described it as "a tiny jewel in an exquisite setting."

In a burst of generosity, Mrs. Barker donated a solid oak door for the parlor. A relic of her grandfather's country home, she and Clay had stored it in their garage, thinking someday they might remodel the entry to their own home.

This wasn't your ordinary panel door. It was solid oak. The carpenter who installed it chose heavy-duty hinges, and when it closed, it was with a firm thud like that of a bank vault. Volunteers sanded and varnished it until it shined like burnished gold.

Then came the gala ribbon cutting with everyone who was anyone as a guest. Yes, they served hot tea and measured the sugar cubes with tiny prongs!

That night, exhausted, Mrs. Barker fell asleep quickly. But about 2:00 AM she woke with a start. "Clay, wake up," she cried, "I have the awfulest feeling. Grandpa's door—we didn't put a lock on it!" Clay rubbed his eyes and mumbled, "So what? The church is locked. No one's going to break in anyways."

"Oh, I don't mean thieves breaking in tonight," she replied. "I mean every Tom, Dick and Harry barging in there and using the parlor whenever they feel like it. I can see teenagers in there with their muddy feet. Or, some of these modern mothers changing their babies, right there on the new sofa. Maybe some of the ushers slipping off in there to smoke, scatterin' ashes on that beautiful new rug."

Would you believe that by noon the next day, Mrs. Barker had herself hired and paid a carpenter to install a dead-bolt lock on that parlor door? "That lock'll keep out anyone—even those on the FBI's wanted list," the carpenter promised as he picked up his tools and brushed off his coveralls.

The next problem was what to do with the keys, there being three of them. A self-appointed committee decided that keys to a place as important as the parlor shouldn't be passed around the members. So they agreed that Mrs. Barker would keep all three, and they themselves would clean the parlor as needed. "We can do it better ourselves," they agreed. "And that way the janitor won't have to say no when someone asks to use the parlor in a way it was never intended to be used in the first place."

Everything went well for several months. The heavy door with its dead-bolt lock stood as a bastion against any who might defame its intended use. Until early fall, that is, when the community garden club held a farewell tea for its president. Although not a church event, all agreed that the club was responsible and "proper." The centerpiece was a lovely arrangement of dried flowers entwining the twin candelabra.

The tea had been over about two hours when the custodian thought he smelled smoke. Sniffing for clues, he saw thin wisps of black smoke oozing from the tiny crack at the bottom of grandpa's oak door. The parlor was on fire! He grabbed the fire extinguisher, then remembered the dead-bolt lock. No chance of getting in. No time to run to Mrs. Barker's home. So he dialed the fire department.

Mrs. Barker, seeing the fire truck speeding toward the church, feared the worst. Not even bothering to put on a jacket, she ran down the sidewalk and arrived at the church just as a husky fireman took careful aim and with one splintering crash chopped down grandpa's door. Once inside, the firemen discovered that smoldering candles had ignited the dried flowers.

The blaze was soon out, but not before soot and smoke and water had blackened the walls and soaked the carpet so that it gave off a squishing noise when Mrs. Barker walked across it, surveying the ruins.

Big tears ran down her cheeks. "This is one of the darkest days of my life," she said to the Preacher, standing helplessly nearby. "All this beauty, all this work, and my precious granddaddy's oak door . . . a shambles, a disgrace, and we worked so hard!"

The next morning, still crestfallen, Mrs. Barker stopped to see Aunt Sarah Biggs, acknowledged as the best Bible student in Tinyburg. Although some jokingly refer to her as "Defender of the faith," they respect her insights into the Scriptures.

"Mrs. Barker, I've been reading my Bible this morning," Aunt Sarah began. "That's my custom, you know. And days when there's trouble, I read extra verses. And do you know that I stumbled onto two amazing verses? Here, read this one in Matthew 16:19 where Jesus said to Peter, 'And I will give unto thee the keys of the kingdom.' And this one from John 10:7 where Jesus said, 'I am the door of the sheep.'"

"Mrs. Barker," Aunt Sarah continued. "You and I've been friends for years—we know every squeaking board in the Tinyburg Church. And I did my part in furbishing the parlor. I donated one of my mother's hand-embroidered scarves for the serving table. But I'm going to level with you.

"I think there's been too many closed doors and too many locks. You can do two things with a lock: you can unlock it to let folks in, or lock it to keep them out. And a door swings two ways—to shut folks out or to welcome them inside. We've been shutting and locking when we could have opened and welcomed. And that's all I've got to say."

If you know Mrs. Barker as I do, you know that she is a strong-willed person. But she's never too proud to admit her own faults. And while Aunt Sarah was quoting Bible verses, it was as if Mrs. Barker saw the whole parlor episode unfold before her eyes, like a movie.

So she rallied the parlor committee and other interested members to pitch in. They shampooed the carpeting, repainted the walls, washed the windows, and sent the furniture out to be refinished.

They searched a long time for a craftsman who could put Grandpa's door back together and refinish it so that it shone again like burnished gold.

When the parlor was reopened, you couldn't tell there had even been a flicker of smoke. But you could see one change: there was no lock on the door.

Instead, neatly lettered on the door was the verse, "I am the door of the sheep." And on one of the inside walls a plaque with the quotation, "I will give unto you the keys of the kingdom."

The next time you're in Tinyburg, stop by the church and see the parlor for yourself. It's a beauty! If the building's locked, Uncle Billy lives just across the street. He keeps a key and will be pleased to show you around.

I understand that through the years, folks who live in Tinyburg often stop by the parlor on a weekday just to be by themselves. It's a quiet, lovely place, almost like a chapel. Brides have been known to slip in there on the mornings of their weddings. The sorrowing have stopped by to get away from the telephone and sympathizers. Couples on the verge of breaking up have come there to sit in silence.

What they're doing is sort of putting the pieces of their lives together again. Or opening new doors of hope. More than one has testified that in so doing, they found the key to a problem they thought was unsolvable.

And if the pieces in your own life are crumbling, ask to be alone a few minutes. Close the door. Read the verses. You may discover the day of miracles is not over!

A Silent Sabbath

No member of the Tinyburg Church is more faithful than Frieda, a gentle and friendly dog, part collie and part shepherd. Frieda belongs to S. Franklin Rodd, a gentleman farmer who lives about three miles from town. Frank, as he's known to his neighbors, attends the rural Ebenezer Church, but Frieda, for some reason, prefers the church in town.

Oh, Frieda doesn't come inside and occupy a pew. But she stations herself near the front door each Sunday morning, wagging her tail at everyone—adults and children, strangers and members. More than one mother has coaxed a sleepy youngster out of bed by saying, "Frieda's up and finished her breakfast, waiting at the church. She'll be disappointed if you're absent."

The boys and girls enjoy petting Frieda and sometimes bring her treats from the breakfast table, such as a scrap of bacon. Her favorite delicacy is waffles, with just a touch of maple syrup. How the kids learned this, I don't know. I do know that more than one family in Tinyburg has a long-standing custom of waffles and syrup for Sunday breakfasts.

For a long time, it was a mystery how Frieda knew when Sunday came. Was it because the Rodds slept later on Sunday mornings, then dressed in their best for church? That couldn't be, because Frieda showed up on Sundays when the Rodds were away on vacation, or maybe snowed in by a winter storm.

Or did she have some unusual sense of time, a seven-day rhythm in her mind that told her it was Sunday?

The local veterinarian came up with the best solution: "I'm guessing it's the church bell. A dog's ears are very sensitive, and she could easily hear the bell, three miles away."

His explanation was verified one weekday when the bell tolled for the funeral of an aged member. This isn't a custom with the Tinyburg Church, but this member had made such a request, which was carried out.

Sure enough, Frieda appeared at the funeral. "That proves it's the bell," observed Uncle Billy Cutrell who, since he lives across the street from the church, keeps track of her coming and going. "I wish all our members were as regular. If anything happens to her, it'll be another funeral around here."

Well, something did happen, but not the way you could imagine. It was a surprise, it was a shock, it was a bolt out of the blue.

Actually, it was a mere piece of paper. But that little scrap of paper was like a match in a dry haystack. It ruffled tempers, raised blood pressures, and kindled emotions. It was a summons, issued by the local justice of the peace. The sheriff delivered it to the home of trustee chairman Burt David:

> Whereas citizen John Gilbert, who lives one block from the Tinyburg Church, has appeared before me, and
> Whereas Mr. Gilbert is employed on the night shift and must sleep in the daytime, and
> Whereas the ringing of the church bell on Sunday mornings is a nuisance, robbing him of needed sleep, and
> Whereas he is asking for an injunction against the church to cease and desist from this aforementioned nuisance,
> I summon your elected officials to appear before me next Monday evening at 7 o'clock to show cause why such an injunction should not be invoked.

Burt David's hands trembled as he read the summons. At the same time, a flush of deep red appeared on the back of his neck near his shirt collar and made its way up to the crown of his bald head.

Nuisance my eye! he said to himself. *Whoever heard of such an adolescent, sophomoric claim that a church bell's a nui-*

sance? The next thing we know, someone will serve an injunction against us for hymn-singing, saying it hurts their ears!

Nevertheless, he called a meeting of the trustees. By the time they met to discuss the summons, Burt had cooled off and warned the committee about doing anything rash:

"After all, our church is a service organization, trying to do good. The last thing we want is a lawsuit. We don't need a public argument with John Gilbert or anyone else. Let's give this a cooling-off period. It won't hurt to go a couple of Sundays without ringing the bell. In a week or so, we can visit Mr. Gilbert, sit down for a man-to-man talk. I think he'll see it our way, and we'll avoid some nasty articles in the *Tinyburg News* as well as back-fence gossip."

The justice of the peace agreed to the delay, and veteran bell-ringer Carl Bradley said he needed to be gone for a couple of Sundays anyway.

And so the next Sunday morning, for the first time in over forty years, the folks in Tinyburg failed to hear the soft and familiar, "Ding-dong, . . . ding-dong, . . . ding-dong." Some of the townspeople paid no notice. Others, who never darken the church doors, looked at their watches as nine o'clock came and passed with no pealing of the familiar bell.

But the biggest disappointment came to the youngsters. Yes, you guessed—Frieda missed Sunday School. She had never been kept away by heat or cold, snow or rain, sleet or storm. But today, silence kept her home, asleep under the back porch at the Rodd farmhouse.

And little treats the kiddies had brought—strips of bacon, dog biscuits, and yes, furtive fragments of waffles—ended up in the garbage.

One three-year-old burst into tears, crying, "I want Feeda, I want Feeda, I want Feeda." But there was no Frieda, and there was no Carl Bradley, his gnarled and arthritic hands gently tugging at the frayed old rope.

Somehow, it didn't seem like Sunday, although the children's choir sang as usual, the Preacher's sermon was typical, and the prayers were just as sincere.

Apparently, the only person pleased with that silent sabbath in Tinyburg was John Gilbert, who slept until noon, uninterrupted, the way he wanted to.

Since Tuesday was Mr. Gilbert's night off, he agreed to meet the trustees that evening. Burt David opened the discussion:

"Mr. Gilbert, our church never intended to be a nuisance. As far as anyone knows you're the only one who's ever complained about the bell. We appreciate your need for sleep. But is it really that much of a problem?"

Mr. Gilbert surprised them with his sharp answer: "You bet that noisy bell's a Nuisance, spelled with a capital *N*. Don't people around here know when it's Sunday? If someone needs a calendar, or maybe an alarm clock, I'll see they get one. A church bell's a hangover from old-fashioned times in the country. Members were scattered, they didn't always know if a preacher would show up for services, so maybe they needed bells. But not today.

"Let me ask you something: If bells are all that important, why not put one on top of the Tinyburg Bank and ring it when the doors open for business? If folks need reminders, put bells on the grocery stores, the service stations. Let's have a bell-o-rama right here in Tinyburg, ringing day and night, seven days a week. Ding-aling, ding-a-ling, ding-a-linga-ding. Ring-a-ling-ding, pussy's in the well. . . ."

"Mr. Gilbert, I think you're being ridiculous," Burt David interrupted.

"Look fellows," Gilbert replied. "I've got a family to feed. The Lord's not going to put food on my table while I'm sitting around in some church house. You do your church business, but you let me have peace to do mine. Good night, gentlemen." And with that, he showed them to the door.

A few evenings later the following letter to the editor appeared in the *Tinyburg News*. When readers noticed it was
signed, "Frieda," they knew it was tongue-in-cheek, but were
fascinated anyway:

> I'm sorry I missed services last Sunday. I missed my little
> friends, waiting in the churchyard like I always do.
> You see, I don't own a watch. And I don't have a calendar.
> They don't make these for dogs.
> So the only way I know it's Sunday is when the church bell
> rings. I may be chasing a rabbit or taking a snooze. But when
> I hear that bell, I take off on a shortcut through the woods,
> and I'm there when the first members arrive.
> It isn't Sunday if the bells don't ring.
> I know this isn't a problem with the rest of you. You can
> keep track of the days and hours without a bell.
> On the other hand, are you sure you don't need a church
> bell? Is something buried deep inside human beings—some
> urge for worship, some feeling of awe and reverence?
> And could it be that man is made so that a pealing bell
> wakens that feeling? Is it a gentle reminder that life is more
> than meat and bread, more than jobs and banks and grocery
> stores?
> You're probably right in guessing that no dog could com-
> pose a letter like this. But you'll have to agree that whoever
> wrote it knew what he was talking about.
>   FRIEDA

With that, I'm bringing this story to a close and allow you,
the reader, to guess how it ended. Did John Gilbert get trans-
ferred? Or break his leg on the job, then change his mind
toward the church when members mowed his lawn and gave
his family a food pounding?

No, it wasn't that simple. To learn if Carl Bradley went back
to ringing the bell, you'll have to visit Tinyburg some Sunday
morning and listen for yourself.

All I'll say is that Frieda's never missed a Sunday since!

Should you need directions, Tinyburg's easy to find. Just
seven miles south of Pretense. You'll know it by the big billboard:

Welcome to Tinyburg—the only city in the United States
with an unlisted zip code!

If you go too far, turn around at the sign, "Resume speed."
Oh, another thing. It's still a secret around Tinyburg who
wrote the letter to the editor and signed Frieda's name.

The Purple Crackerbox

In Tinyburg they call it The Purple Crackerbox, although it isn't a crackerbox. In fact, it's not a box of any kind. It's a one-room barber shop, run by George Mason. It occupies a squat, concrete block building on Main Street, the blocks painted a dazzling purple.

One of the first customers to walk into George's shop said, "Why, this is no bigger than a crackerbox—but whoever saw a crackerbox painted purple?"

"You've just seen one," George replied good-naturedly. "And you've given me an idea. That's what I'm naming my shop, 'The Purple Crackerbox.'"

So when you're in Tinyburg and need a haircut, watch for the funny sign in front of the concrete block building: "The Purple Crackerbox."

George cuts hair for a living, but his hobby is collecting old sayings. On the wall facing the one chair in his shop is a section of chalkboard he salvaged from an abandoned one-room school. Better still, let's call it a blackboard. When George hears an old saying, he writes it on the blackboard, using a variety of colored chalks.

You might wonder what in the world his blackboard has to do with shaves and haircuts. Well, there is no connection, except his customers enjoy reading what he calls his "Old Eddard Sayings." That's a term he picked up in the early days of radio when he listened to Lum Edwards and Ezra Peabody on the popular "Lum 'n Abner" show.

The old sayings also boost his business. Saturday nights, he washes the blackboard and starts a new list on Monday. Some customers come in every week for a trim or haircut—whether they need one or not—just to see what he's come up with.

Through the years, as I've gone to the Purple Crackerbox, I've made a notebook of the sayings I like best:

"If you wash your face in the first frost of the year, you won't have headaches."

"But be careful not to walk in someone's tracks, for if you do, you're sure to suffer headaches all winter."

"If your grandmother visits you on New Year's Day, your chickens will lay better that year."

"If a butterfly lands on you, then you'll get new clothes the colors of the butterfly wings."

"If your shoe comes untied, you'll walk on strange land."

Now should you be interested in marriage, consider the wisdom of these four sayings:

"If you're a woman and curious about whom you'll marry, then eat a baked apple at bedtime and you'll dream about him."

"But if you're a man, look in a well on the first day of May and you'll see the face of your future bride!"

"Be careful not to shake a tablecloth out of doors after sunset, for if you do, you'll never marry."

"To hold on to the woman you love, never sprinkle dust in her shoes, or she'll leave you."

Another one in the same vein goes like this, "Sweep dirt out the door after dark and you'll sweep yourself out of a home."

Now that we know everything about courtship and marriage, turn these four general hints over in your mind:

"If your nose itches, company's coming."

"If you eat pinto or navy beans on New Year's, you'll have plenty of money all that year."

"Don't tell a bad dream before breakfast. If you do, it will come true."

"Smoke follows beauty."

George has also collected a large number of no-no's that bring bad luck:

"It's bad luck to keep two clocks running in the same room."

"It's bad luck to let a newborn baby see the first snow of the year. And it's just as bad to allow any baby to look in a mirror before he's a year old."

"It's also bad luck to cut a baby's hair before his first birthday."

"It's bad luck to look at a new moon through the branches of a tree, to open an umbrella in the house, or for a dog to turn around three times before he lies down."

"If you're leaving on a trip and forget something, it's bad luck to turn around and go back."

"It's always bad luck to break a mirror, to walk under a ladder, or to rock a rocking chair if no one's sitting in it."

"It's also bad luck, when you're visiting a friend's house, to go in one door and leave by another."

Now for a look at eight of George's good luck sayings:

"Nailing a horseshoe over your barn door will bring you good luck."

"Anyone who finds a four-leaf clover is in good luck."

"It's good luck to eat boiled cabbage on the Fourth of July."

"It's good luck to throw a new half-dollar over your left shoulder."

"People who go to bed and get up on the same side of the bed will have good luck all that day."

"Listening to a rooster crow at least three times before you eat breakfast is good for a week of good luck."

"It's good luck to feed farm animals extra rations on Christmas Eve."

"Plant cherry trees on George Washington's birthday and your cherries won't be wormy."

Well, I could go on, for George knows hundreds of witty sayings. But if I give all his secrets, you might not come as often for a haircut!

George has one other tradition. From the Bible, he chooses

and puts on the chalkboard what he calls his "proverb of the week."

"Those other sayings," he explains, "are fun to talk about. But the Bible proverbs, well, they're different. They're just good common sense, what some call 'horse sense.' And they touch on habits a fellow can cultivate, ones that enrich and strengthen life."

Here's the Bible proverb I like best, one he's put on his blackboard many times: "The fear of the Lord is the beginning of wisdom" (Prov. 9:10).

There's little you can do to improve on that advice, which means a healthy respect for God is the kindergarten of life. Whereas scads of folks have all kinds of head-knowledge from textbooks and school rooms, real wisdom begins with putting your life under God's control.

And I guess that's good advice, whether we hear it during a stirring sermon in a magnificent cathedral—or see it on a chalkboard in The Purple Crackerbox on Main Street in Tinyburg.

"Good Morning, Jesus"

George Hunter's the best paperhanger in Tinyburg. Moreover, he's blind. I once asked how, being blind, he could match paper so perfectly.

"Trade secret," he smiled.

His wife estimates the jobs, keeps books, and buys his supplies. His tools are few: a smoothing brush, a trimmer, a braille tape measure, and a small stepladder. Before prepasted paper came on the market, he also needed pasting boards and sawhorses. Now he hand carries his tools from job to job.

The night before George starts a new job, he moves in his tools and gets a mental picture of the layout. His wife will already have sketched each room in braille, showing the door and window openings, appliances, cabinets, and the like. Now he takes his own tape measure and carefully goes around each room feeling the windows, the corners, and the electrical receptacles.

"I never move in on a new job and start it the same day," he once told me. "I size it up the night before. Then, just before I go to bed, I review how each room 'looks' to me. Sort of sets itself in my head. The next morning, I feel like I'm in my own home. I just follow the images in my mind."

Although George's wife is a faithful church member, he seldom attended. That's why it mattered little to him the Sunday the Preacher spoke on "God Isn't a Second Baseman." Several eyebrows were raised when the sermon was announced in the *Tinyburg News*, and Uncle Billy Cutrell said there was an uncommon number of visitors that day.

"I've decided we need a more worshipful spirit," the Preacher began. "More formal and dignified. God isn't a sec-

ond baseman, a fellow we play ball with. He's deity and de-
serves respect. In Old Testament times, the Jews wouldn't even
say the word *God* lest they desecrate the Name itself."

"What I'm getting at," he continued, "is that we must use
languages that befit the occasion. Too much of our praying is
off the cuff. True, God's our Father, but He's not a Daddy or a
Santa Claus!"

The Preacher then revealed a new order of service. A layperson would call on someone for a short invocation. Later, the
Preacher would lead a formal pastoral prayer, or, as he put it,
"one that I've thought through and that's worthy of heavenly
ears."

So armed with a new book, *A Thousand and One Prayers
for All Occasions*, he chose this one for the following Sunday:

> Before the glorious throne of Thy majesty, O Lord, and the
> awful judgment seat of Thy burning love, we, Thy people, do
> kneel with cherubim and seraphim and archangels, worship-
> ing, confessing, and praising Thee, Lord of all, Father, Son,
> and Holy Spirit forever. Amen.

The next week, when Uncle Billy Cutrell stopped to loaf at
the Tinyburg Realty Company, he confessed to Clay Barker
that his own praying days were "about over."

"If I'm gonna start using words like seraphim and archan-
gels, the Preacher can count me out," he continued. "I'll listen
as he prays, but I'm sure not gonna change my ways of addressing the Almighty."

The Preacher himself had some misgivings when it occurred
to him that with a thousand prayers, he had a twenty year
supply. Also it bothered him to think that God had already
read those prayers!

About the third Sunday the Preacher carried his big prayer
book into the pulpit, he was surprised to see George Hunter
sitting on the back pew with his wife. And even more surprised
when George presented himself for membership.

"I've always been a God-fearin' man," he told the congregation, equally surprised. "It's just that since I work alone, I've been one to worship alone. Sunday mornings, by myself, I had my own little devotional at home. Been doing it for years. But I need more: I need companionship, fellowship, or whatever you call it. I need a church family."

The very next Sunday, to the horror of the Preacher, the layperson who was presiding asked George to lead the invocation. Fearing this might embarrass George who was unaccustomed to public worship anyway, the Preacher was halfway out of his seat, hoping to smooth it over and call on someone else. But George was also out of his seat and started on his prayer. Here's what he said:

> Good morning, Jesus! This is blind old Georgie. You know me. I live down here in Tinyburg, 328 Maple Street, just back of the post office. Yellow house with green shutters.

The Preacher, thinking he'd heard everything, sucked in his breath, then let it out with a sigh that could be heard in the balcony. Children snickered, a few teenagers giggled. Most of the adults opened their eyes to see if they were dreaming. But George kept going:

> Guess everything's going well with You, Jesus. Tolerably so with me and the wife. Oh, a fellow always has a thing or two on his heart. But don't want to trouble You. Guess you've got a backlog of complaints, as it is. Sure would like to get this crick out of my neck though, if that's in Your department. I know when I did it. Last Thursday, trying to hang paper around a hot-water heater, I got down on all fours. That didn't do it, so I finally laid down on the floor, flat on my stomach. As I reached around the heater, I felt a pop in my shoulder. I tried liniment, and the Mrs. put a hot water bottle on it, but it's still stiff.

By now the snickering had stopped and a funerallike silence fell on the listening congregation.

> Another thing is that money which Ja, uh, Ja . . . oh, I'd better not say his name right here in front of everybody. But

You know who I mean. Owes me for three rooms and a hall-way of papering. Even had me buy the paper and put it on my bill. I don't want to get mean with him—just need my money.

And yes, I want to thank You for all these nice church folks, the way they took me in. I hardly know how to act in the services. Can't read the words in the hymnbook, couldn't tell you if the Bible begins with Revelation or Genesis. But I understand the Good Book says that love and charity is what it's all about, and I sure feel a roomful of that here this morning.

Well, I'll sign off now. As I said, this is blind old Georgie . . . and it's been real nice talkin' to You.

Collectively, the folks must've used up a big, economy-size Kleenex before George sat down.

The Preacher, deeply moved, like everyone, decided to omit prayer number 798 and went straight into his sermon.

After work the next day, George came by the Preacher's house. "Reverend," he began, "I owe you an apology. It's about that prayer. I don't know the proper words. I just know I was out of place. Maybe you can find something for old Georgie to do besides pray.

"For years, I've prayed at home on Sunday mornings. Just as I imagined what a papering job's going to look like the day before, so I'd sort of visualize God sitting there beside me. And I talk to Him like I would anyone else. But I know that won't do in public."

As best he could, the Preacher assured George that God hears all prayers. "And I want you to know yours touched me deeply," he added.

The reason the Preacher couldn't say more to George was that he was confused in his own mind. He'd been sincere in choosing a prayer style that he thought was meaningful. Now he didn't know. The prayer book on his desk bothered him.

So the next day, which was a Tuesday, the Preacher knocked on the postmaster's office door when he stopped to pick up his mail. The postmaster, a lifelong member of the church, was a practical fellow the Preacher often sought for advice.

"I appreciate your dilemma," the postmaster began. "I also understand where George's coming from. But here's the way I see it. In our business, we see all kinds of mail come through. Some on lilac-scented stationery, written with lavender ink. Some letters addressed on electronic typewriters or by computerized tape. Some postcards are so dog-eared you can hardly read the address. Lots of pieces with no zip code, no street number—just the name and the town, as if our carriers were mind readers.

"But in spite of how the mail's addressed or how it looks, our job is to deliver it. So long as we get the message to where it's intended, we don't worry about the wrappings.

"As I see it, that's what prayer's about. God's not concerned about the envelopes. Some, like George, send their prayers on what we'd call funny-looking stationery. Others send neatly typed prayer letters. But in the end, that doesn't matter."

The Preacher thanked the postmaster, making a mental note to ask someone why they hadn't taught him that in the seminary.

Back in his office, the Preacher concluded that God was big enough to hear any prayer, regardless of the wrappings, and that Tinyburg Church was big enough for *A Thousand and One Prayers for All Occasions* as well as George's petitions.

So, if you should ever visit the Tinyburg Church on a Sunday, you'll be impressed with the pastoral prayer. It will be thoughtful, beautiful, warm, and reverent. Most of all, you'll sense that the Preacher knows God's address. Tinyburg seems to blend with heaven, each time he stands to pray. And occasionally be begins, "Good morning, Jesus, this is the shepherd of the Tinyburg flock."

If you can't visit Tinyburg on a Sunday, then look up George Hunter some weekday and watch him paper a room. His sensitive, almost delicate hands will show you that by the feel of the paper, he knows how to match it.

The same way the Preacher matches Tinyburg with heaven.

The Quilt

For years, Pearl and Ed Ramsey lived on a farm about ten miles out in the country. Until they retired and moved into Tinyburg, they attended the Ebenezer Church, a rural congregation.

The story I want to tell you now took place just before they sold their farm and moved into Tinyburg. One of their daughters, a rather sophisticated young lady by the name of Kay, came home to help them get ready for a yard sale.

"I know we can't move everything to Tinyburg," Pearl sighed as she and Kay sorted dishes, utensils, and linens. "I wish our new house were bigger, so we could just load up everything. But that's out of the question."

"For example, what will I do with my handmade quilts stored in this old cedar chest? Ed and I can never wear them out. Yet I hate to see them go in a yard sale."

One reason Pearl felt this way was that quilt making is as much a wintertime pleasure as flower gardening is in summer. Her neighbors often marveled at her fine stitching, brilliant colors, and original work.

"Now take this one," Pearl said to Kay as she spread a favorite quilt on the bed. "I call this my 'Lifeline' quilt. I made it one winter when you were in junior high school. You were home six weeks with a kidney infection and anemia. The doctor said you needed bed rest, but you helped me cut some of the pieces and sew them into blocks. You remember, don't you?"

"Mother, I'm not sure I do," Kay answered in a tone that suggested she was thinking of something far more important.

You see, Kay has a nice apartment in Bigtown. She tries to

45

say as little as possible to her friends about her roots in Tiny-burg. Unless someone inquires, she never admits she grew up on a farm and, for the first few grades, attended a one-room school.

"Why, Kay, how can you say you don't remember helping me? Look, it's made up entirely of quilt scraps which I saved from your little dresses and play clothes from the time you were a baby. Your life story's here."

"Mother," Kay said condescendingly, "your life may be wrapped up in quilts, but I don't think of my life story in terms of old quilt scraps. I'm living in the present, not yesterday. So let's put that quilt with the other stuff to be sold."

A quick tear came to Pearl Ramsey's eyes, but she quickly brushed it aside when she heard someone at the door. It was Alice, a longtime neighbor who lives at the end of Hubbard's Lane.

Alice hugged Kay whom she hadn't seen since she finished high school. "My, you've done good," Alice said. "We're so proud of you and your job in Bigtown. Understand you live in your own apartment. Your Mom here tells me how pretty it is, the nice furniture you bought. You probably started with more than I've accumulated in forty years of housekeeping."

"Thanks, Alice," Kay answered. "I do like my job, and I've worked hard, decorating my apartment. Some of my friends spend their money on cars and new clothes while I spend mine on furniture. Also, I splurged a little on an interior decorator. But he was worth every cent I paid him. Showed me how es-sential it is to coordinate your color scheme, furnishings, drapes, floor coverings, and the like. He said you can always tell a person's taste by the house they live in. He said that's the difference in living in something that looks like a secondhand furniture store compared to a nice home."

At this remark, Kay's mother dropped her eyes and wiped her hands nervously on her apron. So Alice shifted the conver-sation:

"Why, Pearl, you've laid out my favorite quilt, the one you call the 'Lifeline' pattern. I bet you're fixing to give that to Kay. Lucky girl. I never got anything like that from my Mom. Her house burned about the time I married. Lost everything, including things you can't replace. You know what I mean— old snapshots, keepsakes, souvenirs, hooked rugs, handmade quilts."

"Yes, Mother offered it to me," Kay interrupted. "But I'm limited for space, too. Besides, I use those nice fluffy comforters for cover—you know, the matched sets that go with your drapes and curtains? With central heat, folks don't need heavy quilts anymore. Another thing, I could never stand the smell of mothballs. And you know Mother—she packs everything in mothballs. If Mother really wants me to have this quilt, I suggest she sell it and give me the money. I can use it to apply on a porcelain vase for my dresser. I have one already picked out to match the drapes and comforter."

By this time Alice, a diplomatic person as well as a good neighbor, realized her questions had aggravated a mother-daughter tension she'd been unaware of. So she took another approach:

"Pearl, have you told Kay the full story of her illness, and how you made this quilt? I'll bet you haven't. Well, I'm going to, for I know exactly how it took place.

"When Kay was sick those six weeks, you didn't show your concern very much, but you were worried. That was before the day of antibiotics, and neither you nor the doctor knew what to expect. Fortunately, the bed rest and your good care helped turn her around. But as you sat here by her bed, day after day, sewing those quilt pieces, you designed your own pattern, the 'Lifeline.' You bought bright, red material to connect the pieces you'd saved from Kay's dresses. And you arranged all of it somewhat like the arteries in our bodies.

"You were thinking of rich, red blood. You were thinking of a lifeline for Kay's good health, not a deathblow. And this quilt's the result. It was therapy for you at the time, and, today, it's a memory lane, a lifeline. Kay got well, thank God. Color returned to her cheeks, a color that somehow matched and reflected the colors of this beautiful quilt.

"And you're putting it out in a yard sale for someone who knows nothing about its real value to buy it for a song. Please, please, Kay, for your mother's sake, if no other, don't let her sell that quilt!"

At this point, there was nothing else to say, and the three women sat in silence. Kay picked up a corner of the quilt and fingered it. Pearl continued to twist her apron. Then Alice said it was time for her to go, and that she was real proud she'd gotten to see Kay, and maybe she'd overspoke.

That night when Kay went to bed in her old room, her mother tucked her in, just like when she was a little girl.

"Your dad and I will be moved the next time you come home," Pearl whispered to her. And since the weather had turned unseasonably cold, she reached in the chest for the "Lifeline" quilt and spread it over her and said, "Good night, Kay."

Kay had trouble sleeping. She tossed this way and that. As she fingered her "Lifeline" quilt, she decided to turn on the lamp and look at it more closely. She traced her fingers across the different pieces of beautiful, intricate stitches.

Here were scraps from her baby and doll dresses, some she could barely remember wearing. But the others were familiar—scraps from so many of the home-sewn clothes her mother had made for her. Here was a piece from the dress she wore on her first day at school. Another from a favorite Easter dress. And one from her first formal, pink and white striped dimity with rosebuds and a pink velvet tie belt. Here was her eighth grade graduation dress, a sky blue. And scraps from play clothes, party dresses, but most poignant of all, material from a dress she had worn as the "star" in a school play.

How the memories came back: she was in the fifth grade,

still going to that one-room school before they consolidated with the Tinyburg school system. Her father rigged up some footlights using tin cans for reflectors, and he even made a spotlight, using a piece of bent metal and a 200-watt bulb.

She relived the moment—stepping out on the stage, the footlight blinding her, the spotlight singling her out. It was a magic night of a fairy tale with princesses and princes. Most of it was imaginary and unbelievably amateurish, but the magic was there. And for a few brief moments, she relived that magic as she smoothed out the lines of her mother's "Lifeline" quilt.

The following afternoon, when everything was sorted for the sale, Kay kissed her parents good-bye and started loading her car with what she would keep. Right on top was the "Lifeline" quilt.

"Now, Kay, don't take that old quilt just to please me," her mother said. "You have your own decorating colors. I know it's old-fashioned. I'd rather sell it and give you the money to buy something really nice."

"Mother, believe me, I'm not taking the quilt to please you. I'm taking it to please myself. I've already decided what to do with it. I'll use it for a spread. It won't be packed away and used only for cover during cold weather. I'll use it for a spread, three hundred and sixty-five days in the year. I can make a few changes in my color scheme—a little paint here and there, maybe some new wallpaper with red in it, and it will fit beautifully."

After Kay's car disappeared down the road, Pearl busied herself with washing the supper dishes. As she did so, she hummed to herself:

> Throw out the lifeline across the dark wave,
> There is a brother whom someone should save;
> Somebody's brother! oh, who then, will dare
> To throw out the lifeline, his peril to share?
>
> Throw out the lifeline!
> Throw out the lifeline!

Someone is drifting away;
Throw out the lifeline!
Throw out the lifeline!
Someone is sinking today.
                          EDWARD S. UFFORD

A few weeks later, after Kay had touched up her bedroom, a friend stopped by for coffee.

"I want to show you something really pretty," Kay offered. Then she opened the bedroom door and pointed to the quilt, spread on the bed.

Her friend oohed and aahed, then exclaimed, "Kay, you have a small fortune here! Do you know how much that quilt would bring on the market? It's an original pattern. It's one of the best examples of primitive American folk art I've seen. Works like that can't be duplicated. You can sell that for enough to redecorate your entire apartment."

"But it isn't for sale," Kay interruped.

"Oh, I realize it's not for sale now, but once you get the right price, you can't afford not to sell it."

"It's not for sale at any price," Kay replied. "You see, this is more than a quilt. This is my life. No one sells her life, whether at a yard sale in Tinyburg or at the National Museum of Art."

The Coffee Can

When Pearl and Ed Ramsey retired from farming and moved into Tinyburg, they knew they'd miss the changing seasons of planting and harvesting, the livestock, their longtime neighbors, and fellow members of the Ebenezer Church.

Pearl realized she'd also miss her coffee cans. She owned quite a collection, both in the one-pound and three-pound size.

"Pearl, I believe if you were getting married today, you could start housekeeping with little else than coffee cans," a neighbor remarked one day when Pearl showed off her collection on long shelves on the back porch of their farmhouse.

Like most farm wives of her generation, Pearl made do with odds and ends for many of her household needs rather than running to the store each time she needed something.

For example, Pearl used one can to store buttons of every size and shape and color. Whenever Ed or one of their twin boys popped a button on his jeans or shirts, she could always reach in her coffee can and find an exact duplicate, or one close to it.

Ed used two or three cans himself for nails, screws, nuts and bolts, small tools, and the like. And Bobby and Billy, the twins, each had one can completely filled with marbles. Later, when the grandchildren came along and Pearl learned that plastic spools were rapidly replacing the wooden ones, she saved back one canful of the wooden variety. The grandchildren never tired of dumping the spools out on the floor and playing with them, preferring such to store-bought toys.

Each spring when the Ramseys planted their garden, Pearl had a ready supply of cans to cover the little tomato plants and other tiny vegetables whenever the weatherman predicted frost.

When Bobby and Billy were old enough to go on overnight fishing trips alone, Pearl sent along two or three coffee cans instead of skillets and pans from her kitchen. "You can do lots of things with a coffee can over an open fire," she told them, "such as boiling eggs and potatoes, cooking stew, making hot chocolate, or heating hot water to wash your hands and clean your utensils." Coffee cans held their fishing worms, too.

And when they got their first BB guns, they learned to shoot straight by taking careful aim at the *O* in the word *Folgers* or the *A* in Manhattan.

Hardly a young man from their community went away to military service that didn't receive a batch of Pearl's homemade chocolate chip cookies at Christmas. And—you guessed it—she packed the cookies in a festively wrapped coffee can. "Keeps them fresh and moist," Pearl noted. "Also protects them from crumbling and getting broken up."

It might take me as long as an hour to list all her uses for coffee cans such as picking blackberries, storing ice-cream salt, or using one as a scoop for chicken feed.

But Pearl's pride and joy, on summer Sunday mornings, was to take a bouquet of flowers to the Ebenezer Church, tastefully arranged in a coffee can. If she had time, she might wrap the can in aluminum foil before setting it on the communion table or on top of the piano.

"I look forward to summer," her pastor once said, "because I know you'll be decorating the Lord's house with blossoms from your big flower garden. Pearl, you bring the whole outdoors right inside the church house."

When Bobby and Billy were about ten years of age, they begged their mother not to put aluminum foil around the outside of the cans. "Why in the world do you care, one way or another?" she asked them.

Billy spoke up, "Mom, we sit there and see who can make up the most words from the printing on the labels. You can make up all kinds of words from "Maxwell House" such as "we" and "well" and "ax" and "mouse" and "sell" and even "hell.""

"You mean you sit right there in church and make up bad words off of coffee cans?" she scolded.

"Not always, Mom," spoke up Bobby. "If it's a Folger's can, we can't find many words. What we do is practice spelling the word backwards. We do it back and forth to each other: s-r-e-g-l-o-F. Then F-o-l-g-e-r-s. I can say it faster than Billy. Want to hear me? s-r-e-g-l-o-f, s-r-e-g-l-o-f. s-r-e-g-l-o-f."

"Stop it!" Pearl scolded again. "I don't even care how you spell Folger's frontwards, let alone backwards. If you're determined to make up things to do in church, why not learn a Bible verse backwards? It'd do you more good."

"Oh, Mom, that's old stuff," interrupted Billy. "We already know the Ten Commandments backwards, and some of them mean the same. Want to hear them? 'Thou shalt not kill': kill not shalt thou. 'Thou shalt not steal': steal not shalt thou. 'Honour thy father and thy mother': mother thy and father thy honour. See?

"No, I don't 'see!'" replied their mother. "But what I do want to see is both of you sitting up straight and listening to the minister, not making up nonsense words and turning the Good Book around all crookedwise.

"And another thing—I never want to hear you say h-e-l-l, especially in church.

"The Preacher uses it lots of times in his sermons," replied Billy.

"I know he does. But that's different."

"What's different about it?"

"The difference is why mothers with boys like you turn gray at age thirty-five," she replied.

But those years were gone, and for now, Pearl and Ed's

minds were on their move into Tinyburg . As they reminisced about their sons and the coffee cans—now grown men with families of their own—both wiped tears from their eyes.

"I'll tell you what," Ed promised Pearl, shifting the subject. "Although our yard in Tinyburg will be small, I'll spade up one corner so you can plant a flower bed. Won't be as big as the one you're used to here on the farm, but you can raise enough for an occasional bouquet for the Tinyburg Church. And we don't have to give up all our coffee cans: you'll need something to store buttons and the like, and I'll always need a few nails and screws around the house."

So the following spring after they'd moved, Ed spaded a small flower garden as he'd promised. On Mother's Day, Pearl picked her first bouquet of white daisies, pink peonies, red roses, and sprigs of asparagus fern. "Now Ed, you hold my Bible and Sunday School quarterly while I get out of the car," Pearl said as they pulled up to the curb. "I don't want to spill the water in the can."

How proudly she walked into the Tinyburg Church, clutching her Maxwell House coffee can with its daisies and roses and peonies. It was just like being back in Ebenezer Church.

The only difference was that in her excitement, she'd forgotten the aluminum foil.

So a couple of minutes later as Mrs. Clay Barker walked in, there was Pearl Ramsey actually placing flowers on the altar in a can with big red and black letters: M-A-X-W-E-L-L H-O-U-S-E.

"Pearl, those are mighty pretty peonies," Mrs. Barker greeted her. "But in Tinyburg, we don't bring flowers to church in coffee cans. Now we have some lovely vases in the kitchen downstairs. Let me get one for you. Fact is, my daughter Candice gave the church a beautiful pink, hand-blown glass vase which she bought on a trip to Venice, Italy. It's just made for your flowers."

Ordinarily, Pearl Ramsey is a mild-spoken housewife. But something overpowered her that morning. Maybe it was because she was homesick for Ebenezer Church and her friends there on Mother's Day.

So she surprised even herself when she replied, "But Mrs. Barker, I took flowers to Ebenezer Church for years in coffee cans, and no one complained. Oh, I should have wrapped the can in aluminum foil. I usually do, and there's still time. I'll run home and get a roll."

"Pearl," Mrs. Barker replied icily. "Coffee cans may be OK in little country churches. I belonged to a rural church myself before I married Clay. But, Pearl, *Tinyburg's not Ebenezer*. Coffee cans are out—aluminum foil or no aluminum foil."

"I know it's not Ebenezer as well as you," Pearl shot back. "Would to God it were! But if my flowers and my coffee cans aren't good enough for Tinyburg, then my membership's not good enough. And my offerings aren't good enough. If my peonies and my Maxwell House container leave this church building, I'm leaving. And that's final!"

By now, other members were arriving, and Mrs. Barker dropped the subject as if the president of the United States had suddenly walked in.

The preacher, totally innocent of what was said between the two women, delivered a Mother's Day sermon on the intrinsic value of various gifts, rather than how they're wrapped.

"At Christmas, Mother's Day, birthdays, and anniversaries we share gifts with those we love," he began. "We wrap some in gay, festive gift wrap, tied with bright ribbons and bows. But the gift is what counts, not the package. The same in our Christian lives. Our best gifts to the Lord are personal and from the heart. How they're wrapped means very little."

He then quoted James Russell Lowell:

> Not what we give, but what we share—
> For the gift without the giver is bare.

Next he asked his listeners to turn to 2 Corinthians 8:5. They read in unison, "And this they did, not as we hoped, but first gave their own selves to the Lord."

In conclusion, he quoted Ralph Waldo Emerson:

> Rings and jewels are not gifts, but apologies for gifts. The only gift is a portion of thyself. . . . Therefore the poet brings his poem; the shepherd, his lamb; the farmer, corn; the miner, a gem; the sailor, coral and shells; the painter, his picture; the girl, a hankerchief of her own sewing.

He then called for the closing hymn, and Pearl almost shouted when the congregation sang:

> Here I raise mine Ebenezer;
> Hither by thy help I'm come;
> And I hope by thy good pleasure
> Safely to arrive at home.
> ROBERT ROBINSON

Early Monday morning, Mrs. Barker took a housewarming gift to the Ramseys. "I should have wrapped this and come weeks ago," she apologized as she gave Pearl a handmade afghan. "But after what the Preacher said yesterday, I guess it's the gift that counts, and this is something I made myself."

"That goes for flowers on the altar, too," she continued. "Whether they're in a vase, or a bowl, or a basket or even a coffee can, really doesn't matter. Pearl, forgive me. As long as I'm chairman of the flower committee, you bring flowers just as you always did at Ebenezer. Sometimes I think Tinyburg's getting a little big for its britches, anyway."

With that, both women hugged each other, and, for the moment, Pearl felt all of Tinyburg had turned into a flower garden.

Tinyburg Church enjoys many beautiful traditions. Some say too many. One of the most heartwarming is Pearl's spring bouquet each Mother's Day, carefully arranged in a Maxwell

House coffee can. She offered to wrap the cans in aluminum foil but Mrs. Barker refused:

"Now, Pearl, we want the same Mother's Day arrangement you made at Ebenezer. No cheating. No fudging. No putting on airs."

If you'd like to visit Tinyburg, any Mother's Day is a good time. Always have a big crowd at church. And if the sermon seems too long, you can amuse yourself by making up words from M-A-X-W-E-L-L H-O-U-S-E. Only be careful of the bad words.

Mom's Apron Strings

Cynthia Dunn stood at her front window and peeked through the curtains as she watched the taillights of Ron's car disappear around the corner. Ron, the only child of her short-lived marriage, had just turned sixteen. It was the Saturday night before Mother's Day. Proud of his new driver's license, he was headed for his first dress-up date.

Ron had completed drivers' training in high school. And so long as he had driven around the streets of Tinyburg, or out on the nearby rural roads, Cynthia felt he was safe. But tonight he was driving to Bigtown to pick up his date. And he'd be on the interstate and going through traffic signals, facing traffic you don't see in Tinyburg.

Cynthia fidgeted with her apron strings. The last few minutes hadn't been pleasant. "Ron, do be careful," she'd warned. "There's been so many wrecks this spring. And remember to be home by 11:30. I'll leave a light on. I'll read or do something, but I can't go to sleep until I hear you pull safely into the driveway."

"Oh, Mom!" Ron had replied sharply. "Who do you think I am? Mom's little baby? When are you going to cut those apron strings and treat me like a person with a little common sense of my own?"

It was his remark about the apron strings that brought a catch to Cynthia's throat. She seldom wore an apron anymore, although she had put on a frilly, party apron earlier in the week when she fixed Ron's birthday supper. She wondered where Ron picked up that old expression about "cutting the apron strings." *Teenagers don't talk that way today*, she thought.

After one last look down the now-empty street, she let the curtain fall back into place, then started for the kitchen. She was making miniature corsages for some of the older mothers in the Tinyburg Church. It would help pass the time until Ron got home.

Then her eyes rested on the top of the piano, where in a triple frame she had displayed her favorite photos of Ron. First, of course, was his baby picture, his eyes already flashing the impish look of his daddy. The other was his six-year birthday photo, showing him in a cowboy suit with Texas boots and a bandanna. How proud he'd been of that outfit, wearing it until it was threadbare, sometimes sleeping in it. The third was his junior class photo. How mature and grown-up he appeared. How quickly the years had passed, changing her baby boy into a man.

As she sorted the ribbons, rosebuds, May daisies, and asparagus fern at the kitchen table, she scolded herself for worrying about Ron.

She remembered the summers he had spent at her parents' farm home, helping his Grandad run the tractor, learning to swim in the stock pond, building strong muscles as he worked in the hay. Why, he could have driven a car when he was thirteen, if the law had permitted. And he wasn't a show-off. But still, you read all those horror stories in the newspapers about teenage drinking, drag racing, and the like. She trusted Ron—but what if other kids pressured him?

The busy boulevards of Bigtown were not the tree-shaded, peaceful streets of Tinyburg.

"I don't care about the car," she told herself. "It's insured and one can always buy another one, or patch up the wrecked one. But it's not possible to breathe life back into the crushed and mangled body of your own son."

She shuddered as she thought of some of the accident photos she'd seen in newspapers and magazines lately.

As she twisted and intertwined the ribbons among the fresh

flowers on her kitchen table, Ron's comment about apron strings came back to her. And like an old movie playing before her eyes, she recalled her own childhood on the farm, her mother busy with children and chores, usually wearing an apron. She and Cynthia's dad still lived on the family farm, about twenty-three miles southwest of Tinyburg.

"She was always on old-fashioned kind of Mother," Cynthia whispered, as if talking to the flowers in front of her. "Even wore a freshly starched apron to her country church at Ebenezer when we children were small. She often said she felt half-dressed without an apron."

As she assembled the corsages, Cynthia continued to visualize those childhood scenes in which her mother appeared, wearing an apron. And for many reasons other than keeping her dress clean.

While working in the kitchen on a hot day, an apron was handy to wipe the perspiration from your face and eyes. And if you needed to wash your hands in a hurry, an apron could also double as a towel. Cynthia could also see her mother fanning herself with her apron, or using it to scare the cats out of the kitchen, or to shoo flies off the supper table. Her apron often doubled as a hot pad, when she picked up steaming pots and pans from the stove or oven.

If she saw company coming unexpectedly down the line, she might swish through the house, using her old apron as a dust-rag to tidy up the furniture (always slipping on a fresh apron before they arrived!).

She sometimes made a quick sling out of her apron to carry one of the babies, or to enfold one of the children when they ran into the house scared, or hurting with a stumped toe. And if they cried, the soft folds of Mother's apron gently dried the tears away.

Her mother owned one or two dressy aprons for Sunday guests. But mostly, she wore everyday aprons made from sugar and feed sacks carefully saved during the 1940s.

Cynthia remembered a summer revival when they were late finishing their chores, and rushed to get ready. Her mother was embarrassed when she got to church, for she looked down and saw she was still wearing the same wet and stained apron she'd worn that day to can peaches. Still, she sang as determinedly as ever:

> I am bound for the promised land,
> I am bound for the promised land;
> O who will come and go with me?
> I am bound for the promised land.
> SAMUEL STENNETT

"Mother wouldn't let a little thing like a dirty apron keep her from climbing Jordan's stormy banks to reach the glory land," Cynthia smiled to herself.

Working in the garden, Cynthia's mother often gathered up the corners of her apron and used it as a pouch while she picked peas, corn, and tomatoes. Or in the henhouse and orchard, she did the same as she gathered eggs and picked blueberries and apples.

She kept a small, sharp knife in the pocket of her apron, which came in handy as she sat under a willow tree in the backyard, trimming carrots or peeling potatoes. And once the vegetables were ready, she gathered the corn shucks, bean pods, and peelings in her apron, then dumped them in the chicken pen for the rooster and his harem to pick over and scratch around in.

If she were in a hurry to feed cracked corn to the chickens, she might scoop up a half peck or so in her apron, then scatter it with her hands.

Before she knew it, Cynthia was daydreaming about the simple farm life of her childhood, back when something as ordinary as a woman's apron was as essential as butter on a hot biscuit.

Then a jab of memory cut across her mind like the switch

her mother sometimes cut off the willow tree and applied to her bare legs. It was the day a neighboring family invited her to go with them to the county fair in Tinyburg. Cynthia was about ten, old enough to go places with friends, but her mother said, "No." Maybe it was because Tinyburg was twenty-three miles away, a long distance in those days. Cynthia couldn't remember why, but she could remember how it hurt. Oh, not so much missing the fair, but what her little friend said, in a teasing, mocking tone of voice:

"What's the matter, Cynthia? Still tied to your Mommie's apron strings?"

Even now the memory of those words cut into Cynthia's heart.

The corsages finished, Cynthia wrapped them carefully in a plastic bag and put them in the refrigerator. She hoped the older mothers and grandmothers would get as much pleasure wearing them as she did in making them.

By now it was 10 o'clock, an hour and a half before Ron was due home. The old worries crept back into her mind, gnawing like hungry rats.

Then on an impulse, she did something that surprised her. Removing the apron she'd been wearing to arrange the flowers, she cut off both strings, then hung them on Ron's bedroom doorknob.

After watching the ten o'clock news, she turned off all the lights except the one in the hallway, and pretended to go to sleep.'

"By the way, what time did you get home last night?" Cynthia asked Ron at breakfast the next morning.

"Oh, it was a little before midnight. Didn't you hear me?"

"No, I went to bed early," Cynthia replied. "Guess I dozed off." She knew this wasn't the whole truth but felt confident she could be forgiven for a white lie, especially on Mother's Day.

"Another thing," Ron continued. "What's the deal about

that apron, you know, with strings cut off, hanging on my door? Some kind of joke?"

"Not a joke, Son. Far from it. More like a puzzle. If you can't solve it now, wait a few years. When you're a parent, you'll understand."

Later that morning at the Tinyburg Church, the older women beamed as they stood at the front while Cynthia pinned a corsage on each, followed by a hug and kiss.

For his Mother's Day sermon, the Preacher told about the miracle of healing, from the nineteenth chapter of Acts. These miracles took place during the ministry of the apostle Paul, when at one time handkerchiefs or aprons carried from him to the sick resulted in their healing through the patient's faith in God.

"A generation ago, aprons were common in our homes," the Preacher noted. "They sort of symbolized the love of a mother, as well as serving utilitarian purposes. Aprons may be old-fashioned today, but the old-time love of parents and children are just as modern as laser beams and computers."

At this point Ron, who was singing in the youth choir, caught his mother's eyes in the congregation and flashed her a big smile.

It reminded her of his baby picture, and of her own mother shelling peas in the backyard. Most of all, it reminded her that we never outgrow the pleasure and need of love.

The Steeple

Years ago, long before he was elected county tax assessor, S. Franklin Rodd drove in to Tinyburg one Thursday morning to talk with the Preacher.

"Preacher," he began, "you don't know me very well since I live on a farm and attend a little rural church. Right now, we're without a pastor, but I've got to talk to someone. At times, I feel like I'm losing my senses . . . can't sleep, can't keep my mind on my work."

When the Preacher asked how the problem started and how long he'd been bothered, Mr. Rodd continued:

"You may remember reading in the *Tinyburg News*, about eight months ago when our fourteen-year-old son, Frank, Jr., lost his eyesight in a hunting accident.

"What bothers me is why God would let a thing like this happen to a good boy like Frankie? Oh, I know how the accident happened. And if I'd been with him that morning, I could have prevented it. But I want to know why? Where was God that morning or His angels? Frankie never gave me and his mother no worry of any kind. He likes school, gets along well with his friends, helps me on the farm, takes an interest in his 4-H projects. Now that he's blind, he'll never be able to drive a car, watch television, enjoy a beautiful sunset, or even see his own children. I don't wish no harm on anybody else's kids, but I know some teenagers who're always in some kind of trouble. Why couldn't it have been one of them?

"Oh, I know it's not right to think such things, but Preacher, I'm being honest, just leveling with you about these terrible thoughts that come to me, especially at night when I can't sleep.

64

"Oh, Frankie, he's adjusting, He's learning to cope, and his attitude's good. But it's me. I guess I'm mad at God. Preacher, you're a man of the Book. You studied theology and all that. Tell me, why does God allow bad things to happen to good boys like Frankie?"

At this point, Mr. Rodd gripped his fists so tightly that his knuckles turned white, and he kept biting his lips to keep them from quivering.

For a minute, the Preacher dropped his head, his chin resting on his chest, as if he were praying. Then he answered, softly and deliberately, almost a word at a time:

"Frank, if I could tell you why all the bad things happen, I'd be the wisest man in the world. You've asked the hardest question anyone ever thinks of—why bad things happen to good people. At the same time, good things happen to bad people.

"The Book of Job in the Old Testament, which is the oldest book in the Bible, wrestles with that question. Job's seven sons and seven daughters died in a terrible storm. Then Job lost all his property, went bankrupt, even lost his health. And he asked why? Why? Why? I'm not sure Job ever got the answer he was looking for. I do know he got to where he could say, with faith, "For I know that my redeemer liveth. . . . I have heard of thee by the hearing of the ear: but now mine eye seeth thee."

"Mr. Rodd, all of us have heard about God. But not everyone sees and knows Him in a personal way. Sometimes it takes the darkness to bring out the light."

Mr. Rodd replied to the Preacher that those were pretty words, but the hurt was still there, and he still wondered why.

Changing his approach, the Preacher stood to his feet and suggested, "Frank, let's go downtown for a walk. Maybe I can show you what I'm trying to say but can't find the words."

Since only 1,473 people live in Tinyburg, one doesn't walk far in any direction until there's no place else to walk, except down the highway. So the two made a big circle of the town.

After walking a few minutes in silence, the Preacher spoke as they passed the high school:

"Frank, although Tinyburg's a small place, it's big enough to answer nearly all the questions that folks around here ask, including the basics. Who? What? How? When? Where? Take schools here in Tinyburg: they can show a fellow how to do nearly anything.

"Starting with the elementary grades, the faculty members teach the youngsters how to read, how to spell, how to write, how to do simple math. As they reach higher grades, the youngsters learn how to do experiments in the chemistry lab, how to use computers, how to play band instruments and sing in choruses, how to play basketball and soccer, how to do auto repairs, even how to cook. In universities, young people train to be airline pilots, attorneys, teachers, dentists, architects, engineers, astronomers—nearly anything you can think of.

"But, Frank, there's one question our schools in Tinyburg can't answer. And you won't find the answer in the biggest university in the world, either. That's the question of why Frankie's blind. The most learned professors with their long, black robes and impressive degrees can't tell us why. All they can explain is how."

The two men walked on down the street in silence until they passed the weekly newspaper, *Tinyburg News*.

Again the Preacher spoke. "Now, Frank, whenever you have a 'what' question, that is, 'What's happened?' you can most often find the answer here in this newspaper office. You can go through the files and read about local, national, and world events. Newspapers tell us the facts about life in general— what team won the World Series, how candidates fared in various elections, snowstorms and tornadoes, business and finance, births, deaths, accidents—you could find the story about Frankie losing his eyesight in one of the back issues.

"Ours is a small newspaper. If you go to a library and consult big daily papers such as the *New York Times*, you'd find a record of nearly everything. Whatever happened, it's recorded in newsprint. But, Frank, the most prestigious newspaper in the world can't begin to tell you why Frankie's blind."

The walk continued until they reached the county court-house. Again, the Preacher did most of the talking. "Now inside these offices are detailed records about who's lived and died in this county for generations. Tells when they were born, who they married, the property they bought, when they died. Add these records to the city directory and the phone directory, and you've got most of the answers to the 'who' of life.

"But, Frank, although these records tell you 'who,' they can't tell you why Frankie's blind."

Again the two men made their way up and down the streets of Tinyburg, the Preacher and S. Franklin Rodd, probing the eternal question, "Why do bad things happen to good people?"

About that time they passed the offices of an automobile club. "Frank, if you and I stopped here, we could find the answer to nearly all the 'where' questions that folks ask. They've got maps from all over. They show where the rivers and creeks and lakes and railroads are, as well as the highways, plus every town and city and village.

"Over at the library, we could find world maps and atlases that tell where all the countries and oceans and seas are as well as their states, cities, and towns. No one need be ignorant of where anything in this world can be found. It's all mapped and spelled out.

"But, Frank, the most detailed map in the world can't tell you why your fourteen-year-old son is blind for life. You may be tired, but let's move on."

Just then, the town clock struck eleven o'clock. The Preacher looked up to the two hands that had marked the minutes and hours as long as anyone could remember. "That old clock knows all the answers about 'when,'" the Preacher observed.

"Summer and winter, spring and fall, night and day—it keeps right on telling us when things take place.

"Whether it's a pocket watch, alarm clock, or town clock, most of us depend on them to tell us when to get up, when to eat breakfast, when to go to work, when to take a nap, when to get the mail, when to go to bed. For generations, people have been fascinated by when things happen. You hear about a new baby, and right away you ask when it was born.

"Frank, that clock ticked away the morning your Frankie was in that hunting accident. It recorded the 'when.' But as you know, the most expensive timepiece in the world or the most accurate or the fanciest can't tell more than 'when' something took place."

By now, the men had covered the five questions, Who? What? When? Where? and How? Still, the question of questions went unanswered—the one Job asked, the one everyone eventually asks: Why?

The Preacher and Mr. Rodd had by now made a complete circle of Tinyburg and were back at the church where they'd started. Mr. Rodd turned to get in his car, saying he had to get back to the farm.

"Wait, Frank," the Preacher cautioned. "We still haven't answered the big question. And I can't promise you that I ever can. But take off your hat and look at the steeple on our church. That's right, lean way back until you can see the very tip end, up where the weather vane's fastened on.

"That old steeple's been there through thick and thin, war and peace, depression and prosperity, famine and plenty. Two or three times it's been struck by lightning. Once a strong wind toppled it over. But each time, our members agreed that we might give up lots of conveniences, but not that steeple. We could do without pews, air conditioning, a pulpit stand, or an organ far better than we could do without that steeple."

"How's that?" Frank asked.

"Oh, a steeple takes our eyes off ourselves. When you look at a steeple, it sort of lifts your heart right on up into the heavens.

"As long as folks are looking up, you can't keep them down. Life needs a lift. We need a vision. We need the upward look. And, Frank, whenever I look at that steeple, it's like a giant hand pointing to God.

"One other thing, Frank. Look at that weather vane, too. Never stays long in the same direction. Always changing with the wind, pointing to the northeast, then to the north, and maybe the next day to the south. And I see a message there, too. For I'm reminded that whichever way the wind blows, God is love. God's not wishy-washy: He's not fickle and changeable, like the weather."

It was about dinner time, and Frank felt much better as he drove home. He turned on the car radio to hear the farm roundup at noon, one of his favorite programs, which ends with a thought for the day. Here's what the announcer said, "You can't turn back the clock. But you can wind it up again."

As he swung into the driveway and saw Frankie romping with his favorite collie, Frank thought how badly he'd like to turn back the clock to when his son could see: "I'm not going to allow my mind to dwell on such negative thoughts. I'll wind up the clock for today. I'm going to look up, to be a steeple person."

If there's time when you visit Tinyburg, park your car, get out, and go for a walk past the high school where they tell you "how." And the newspaper office where they tell you "what." And the courthouse where they tell you "who." And the town clock which tells you "when." And the automobile club whose maps tell you "where."

But regardless, stop at the Tinyburg Church and look up at the steeple and weather vane. You may discover a ray of hope for some deep, dark, question mark of "why?" that's plagued you for years.

A Perfect Marriage

Mr. and Mrs. Clay Barker and their daughter and son-in-law, Candice and Ted Spiller, are what you'd call pillars of the Tinyburg Church. A close-knit family, their lives revolve around church and home and community.

But as in all families, they struggled over some rough ground which they're glad is in the past.

Take Candice and Ted's marriage, for example. The first five years were hectic, bringing them to the brink of breaking up. As they review those years, they smile at their immaturity. At the time, however, it wasn't funny. Let me explain.

On the surface, they appeared to enjoy a perfect marriage. After a family dinner noting their fifth anniversary, their two mothers were washing dishes in the kitchen. Mrs. Barker said to Carl's mother, "You can't imagine, Mrs. Spiller, how proud I am to rear a girl like Candice. I've never heard her say one cross word to your Ted."

"I'm like you," replied Mrs. Spiller as she dried the last of the silverware, "for Ted has never said an unkind word about Candice, at least around me. Of course I reared him that way. He never talked back to me like some boys do, especially in their teens."

The truth is that in those early years, Ted and Candice *didn't* raise their voices to each other. Fact is, Candice didn't speak negatively about anyone.

The habit that did hurt Candice in those years was writing notes. She just loved to write. The only thing was: her notes were picky. If she didn't like the July 4 picnic, she wrote the city council. If the garbage trucks made too much noise, she wrote a letter to the editor of their local newspaper.

If her kids got bad grades at school, she wrote the teachers to remind them of their poor judgment.

Usually, Candice was correct. "Lots of things in this old world need straightening out," she told a neighbor. "So I keep my eye open to the faults of folks. Figure I do them a favor when I correct them."

She designed her own note cards, edged in black. Neatly lettered at the top were four words, "Candid Notes from Candice." One recipient said they reminded him of death notices!

If the Preacher wasn't too sheepish to admit it, he could tell you a story or two about Candice's candid notes. The first Sunday he was in Tinyburg, Candice pressed a note in his hand after the sermon. Not bothering to look, the Preacher assumed that here was a generous member who had given him a $5 bill (maybe even $10 or $20), somewhat like a tip.

He had good reason to think so. In his last pastorate, one member gave him a piece of paper money every Sunday. Didn't believe in church budgets. The Preacher soon learned that the hotter he blistered the congregation, the bigger the tip.

Although he doesn't like to admit it, the Preacher got desperate at the end of one month when a car payment came due, and he was short of funds. Since his benefactor disliked Sunday baseball—thinking it caused most of the evils in the world—the Preacher toyed with the idea of an entire sermon on the perils of Sunday sports. At first, he dismissed the idea, not wanting to "preach for money."

But the more he thought about it, the worse the evils of Sunday ball playing appeared. So although he faced a little problem of finding a text, he relented. Sure enough, he was rewarded with a $50 bill in the palm of his hand.

You see, therefore, why the Preacher speculated that Candice could be another generous member who preferred to give in cash. But when he got home and reached in his pocket, he found instead one of Candice's notes:

Dear pastor: Welcome to Tinyburg. In college I majored in theater and drama. Too, I made good grades in grammar. Each Sunday—as a help to you—I will keep a list of your grammatical errors and mispronounced words. Today's list numbers 27 errors. If you will file these notes and review them, you can improve. Please don't get discouraged. Our last pastor made 37 errors in his first sermon, which he later reduced to an average of only 9 per Sunday. (Signed) Candice Barker Spiller.

Candice also wrote notes to her husband. "Ted, dear," began her first note, soon after their honeymoon. "Toothpaste comes with a little round cap. It screws on the end. When finished, turn the cap clockwise. Firm, but don't force it. This way, the toothpaste won't dry out."

Week after week, for five years, the notes continued. Ted, being conscientious, saved all of them in a shoebox, then found even bigger boxes. Occasionally, he reviewed them, seeing how he might improve.

But lest you judge this marriage as one-sided, let me tell you how Ted handled his frustration. He did so by complimenting a third person such as his mother. If he were out of clean shirts he might say, for example, "Candice, when I was growing up, Mother even ironed my underwear, folding and arranging my handkerchiefs and socks in neat stacks in my drawer. Why, I could have dressed in the dark. I always knew where everything was—and never ran out of something clean to put on."

The next morning Ted found this note in his dresser. "Ted dear, I have an idea how we can save on our electric bill. On winter mornings when you get up first, please don't turn on any lights. Just dress in the dark."

One day at lunch when Candice had burned the corn bread, Ted observed, "You know, Candice, when I was growing up, I never realized what a good cook mother was."

That happened to be Ted's night for bowling. Although he

got home a few minutes late, he was surprised to find their bedroom door locked. He was more surprised to find this note on the door: "Ted dear, why don't you just sleep on the couch in the den? It's more comfortable. And really, it wouldn't be worth your while to come to bed at this late hour."

The next morning at the breakfast table, Candice noted that she was doing poorly on her diet and she couldn't bring herself to step on the scales. Ted made no comment until he looked out the window and saw Joan, their neighbor, jogging down the street. "Candice," he said, "have you noticed how trim Joan keeps herself? Always out early, jogging. Gets home in time to fix a nice breakfast. Always making those low-calorie desserts and salads."

"My mother was that way," he continued. "Never allowed herself to get overweight as she grew older. Truth is, all the time I was growing up, she set a good table. She worked at it. Took home extension courses in nutrition, food preservation, and home decorating."

That night in his dresser drawer Ted found another note:

"Ted dear, I have a wonderful idea. You must write a book. The title can be *When I Was Growing Up*. The theme: If you've got a good mother, why gamble on marriage? It should be a best-seller!"

And so it went, back and forth, tit for tat, year after year. Never an open hostility. Just third-person compliments and candid notes.

It reached a climax, however, about six months after their twenty-fifth anniversary. That summer, Candice substituted in the Tinyburg Bank for a friend who took an extended vacation out West. She enjoyed the work, met new people, picked up some extra dollars.

Her last day on the job, Candice typed this note: "Ted, dear, until I worked at the bank this summer, I had no idea that most men in Tinyburg make considerably more money than you.

And, dear, I want you to know I won't be lonesome if you get a second job—maybe nights or weekends. I know you love me, Ted, and you want me to have nice things like other wives in Tinyburg."

The next morning Ted threw some extra clothes in the car and drove off. Didn't know where he was going, or when he'd be back. Just knew he didn't want any more notes in his dresser drawer. And he presumed Candice had her fill of Mother Spiller, too.

The last thing he did was dump the big box of notes in the backyard and set them afire. A few minutes later, while gassing up at a service station, he heard the fire siren. Ted's curiosity grew to alarm when the fire truck headed toward his neighborhood. Racing home, Ted found that his little bonfire had spread into the grass, then to the garage which was now ablaze. Candice drove up about the same time. Although the flames were quickly doused, Candice didn't wait for her pencil to speak her mind. Neither did Ted reply with a roundabout story of his mother. All he said was, "Candice, I lit the match, but both of us have been building that fire for a long time."

With that he drove off, deaf to Candice's questions as to when he'd be back except to say, "Maybe never."

Candice, depressed, wondered whom she could turn to. Not to either mother, for both knew this was a perfect marriage. Then she thought of Anna, her washerwoman, who came every Thursday to clean and do the laundry. Anna, with little formal education, lived a plain and ordinary life. Yet she always hummed as she went about her work. Nothing seemed to get her down. Candice wanted her secret.

Anna invited Candice to sit in her porch swing. She thought a long time after Candice told her problems, then said: "I guess it all goes back to what my daddy told me years ago. He said Anna, there's enough bad in the world to keep a body depressed all the time. But there's also enough good to keep us smiling. He said I could grovel around in the garbage like a pig, looking for something rotten to criticize. Or I could spend my time looking for the good in folks.

Daddy also said to walk on the sunny side. So even if it's hot weather, and I have a choice of a shady or a sunny side of the street, I take the sunny side. And another thing, I carry this clipping, "The Garden," with me. Cut it out of the *Illinois Baptist* years ago. Here's my favorite part:

> . . . . and so with love, for love aims to please the beloved, not to reform. We can no more make someone good than we can make bluebells bloom in a blizzard. What we can do is love them through the gates of happiness. And the wonder is that when folks are happy, they are more likely to be good. This is the secret of the garden, this is the miracle of love.

I'll not go into detail about the next couple of days . . . Ted's phone call . . . Candice's willingness to see herself in Anna's advice . . . the reunion and homecoming.

What I will detail is what happened since. Ted never did get around to writing that best-seller. Seldom even talks about growing up. And Candice decided to use her old candid notes for scratch paper. Oh, she still writes. But she has new, lilac-scented stationery. "Love notes from Candice" is the heading, plus a color print of a bed of petunias in the lower left corner.

She's always leaving little love notes where Ted can find them—on the mirror, the refrigerator door. And when Ted brags on his mother, he goes to her house to do so.

Should you wish to visit the Spillers, a good time is some summer morning when the flowers are in bloom. Candice planted a flower bed just about the spot of the bonfire. She likes to take her coffee out there on summer mornings and write notes. And to reread "The Garden"—especially the line, "We can no more make someone good than we can make blue-bells bloom in a blizzard."

And the Preacher? Well, his grammar's about the same although the content seems to improve every Sunday. And even the old-timers say it's been ages since he preached on Sunday baseball.

The Yellow Tights

As a little girl growing up in Tinyburg, Candice Spiller was always giving recitations, taking part in school and church plays, and even staging her own Little Miss America pageant.

It should have been no surprise, then, that her first daughter, Rhonda, was quite a show-off. After seeing her first circus at the age of three, Rhonda attempted to put on a lion show, using five little kittens, barely old enough to have their eyes open. But alas, the kittens wouldn't cooperate, clawing and scratching their way out of cages fashioned from cereal boxes.

At an early age, Rhonda learned to stand on her head in the corner of a room, balancing her little legs against the wall to steady herself. And in the summer months, she did cartwheels by the hundreds in the backyard.

So when a tumbling and gymnastics class was formed on Saturday mornings at the junior high school gym, Rhonda begged her mother to go.

"But Rhonda, you're still in kindergarten," Candice replied. "You can't keep up with the bigger kids in that class."

"I can too," Rhonda cried, stomping her foot with each word, a habit which both parents had tried unsuccessfully to break. And when the instructor pointed out that children should begin training while they're young and agile, Candice gave in and enrolled her for a twenty-six-week course.

Her daddy, Ted, took her on a shopping trip to Bigtown to pick out a pair of tights. Instead, they came home with two pairs. One pair, gray with navy blue trim, was to wear to Saturday classes. She chose a second pair, bright yellow with green trim, to wear at exhibitions.

"When Rhonda steps out on the gym floor, she'll look like a canary out of a cage, instead of a gymnast," Candice noted. "And even the kindergarten boys will line up to watch her perform."

Although naturally poised like her mother, Rhonda grew even more so. Having decided she was too grown-up to sit with her parents during services at the Tinyburg Church, she insisted on sitting down in front with three of her little friends. Their favorite pew was the second from the front in the middle section.

"Now if you sit there, I don't want you giggling and whispering, or making paper dolls out of your Sunday School papers," warned Candice. "Listen to the Preacher and pay attention."

"I hear every word he says," Rhonda replied in a grown-up tone of voice. "Oh, sure," Ted answered. "Probably could recite his sermon backwards to him. But your mother and I will be pleased if you remember the first five minutes."

On a bright October Sunday morning, Rhonda begged to wear her yellow and green tights to Sunday School. "You mean wear them right into the church house, just like you were stepping out on a gym floor?" Candice replied in a shrill voice. "Are you out of your mind? That's the Lord's house, not a three-ring circus.

"And another thing. When Jesus was a little boy, He went to the Temple with His parents. Do you think He dressed up like a circus clown?"

"I'll bet He didn't wear braces on his teeth, either, and I know two boys who come to our church with braces. And look at all the pretty yellow leaves on the trees. God made the leaves. He wouldn't care if I wear yellow tights," said Rhonda.

"Well I care," Candice answered in desperation. "You're not going to wear yellow tights in church and make a monkey out of yourself. And that's that!"

"Then I'll wear my long granny dress," Rhonda replied, matter of factly.

"Now you're being sensible," Candice answered. "My mother always told me that if girls wore longer dresses to church, everyone would listen more to the preacher."

That morning in church, Ted and Candice watched proudly as Rhonda walked down to her favorite pew with her three little friends. She looked so prim and proper in her granny dress. And although they knew she and her friends probably didn't hear a half dozen words of the sermon, at least they weren't squirming and giggling.

The Preacher was really wound up that October morning. He had attempted, unsuccessfully, to launch a visitation program. He'd tried everything. Typed prospect lists, put up posters and goal boards, passed out assignment cards, printed announcements in the bulletin. But no one would budge. It was as if the members were glued to their pews, satisfied with those who had enough initiative on their own to attend the services.

So this morning, he decided to pull out the stops and really lay it on the members for their unwillingness to get out and visit.

"Jesus told us to go out into the highways and hedges," he began. "Jesus told us He came to seek and save the lost. He commanded us to go into all the world, and that includes Tinyburg. But no one pays Him any mind. We listen, but do nothing.

"Friends, if Jesus asked us to stand on our heads for Him, I say we should be willing to try, even if we fall flat on our faces. And another thing. . . ."

At this point, the Preacher hesitated, sensing he had lost his audience. Every eye was glued on the second pew from the front, in the middle section, where Rhonda sat and her three little friends. Only now, Rhonda was no longer sitting. She was standing on her head in the pew! Yes, standing on her head in plain view of everyone. And the long granny dress had fallen down to her waist, revealing her bright yellow and green tights. Had she been swinging on a trapeze bar, she would have attracted no more attention.

The congregation sat speechless, mesmerized by her slender legs and pointed toes. Then someone giggled, and another laughed, and the spell was broken as the congregation roared.

Rhonda, apparently innocent in what she had done, wore a puzzled look on her face. The Preacher, having lost his place in his sermon, fumbled with his notes. Finally he continued, "And as I was saying, if Jesus asked us to stand on our heads. . . ."

By now Candice had heard all she wanted to hear about standing on your head for Jesus. Marching down to the front, she motioned for Rhonda, grabbed her sharply by the arm, and marched her outside.

Driving home, she was too angry to say anything. Once inside the house, she exploded with the fury that only a combination of embarrassment, shock, and disbelief can trigger.

"Rhonda Spiller," she began, "not only did you embarrass me and your daddy by putting on a sideshow in front of our church friends. You also disobeyed me by wearing those tights."

"But Mother, I wore a long dress so no one could see. And how did I know the Preacher would ask us to stand on our heads?"

"Silly girl, he didn't ask anyone to stand on their heads. He only said that if Jesus asked us, we should. But I've never read in the Bible where Jesus commanded anyone to stand on their head. The Bible's a religious book, not a training manual for sideshow freaks."

"I'm no sideshow freak," Rhonda answered, stamping her foot to emphasize each syllable. "I just did what the preacher said to do. It was like our teacher in gym giving us instructions."

"You did what you *thought* he said to do—and don't stamp your feet again, ever! His statement about standing on your head was just an illustration, to get people's attention."

"You mean he didn't mean what he said?" Rhonda asked.

"Forget it," Candice replied. "Forget all about gym class, yellow tights, standing on your head, what the Preacher meant or didn't mean. Change into your play clothes and get ready for lunch."

By now Ted, who stayed until the service ended, was coming up the front steps. Candice met him at the door, where Rhonda couldn't hear: "What did you think?"

"I wouldn't tell Rhonda," he replied with a grin, "but I thought it was one of the funniest things ever. I'll never forget it, nor will I forget the Preacher's sermon. With Rhonda's help, he really made his point."

On visitation night that week, the Preacher was surprised when twenty people showed up to make calls. "You good people made more visits tonight than in the past six months," he beamed when they returned for coffee and a report meeting. "Think I'll preach more often about standing on your head for Jesus."

Rhonda still wears her long, granny dress to Sunday School on special occasions. But not until Candice raises her skirt for a last minute inspection, to see what she's wearing underneath.

And it's sort of a standing joke around the Tinyburg Church that whenever the Preacher's pushing some important project, or wishes to emphasize an announcement, he begins by saying, "Now I don't expect any of you to stand on your heads, but I do wish you'd. . . ."

Inevitably, he gets better than usual cooperation.

Someday, I hope you'll visit Tinyburg. Folks there do things a little differently. But it's refreshing to be around people unafraid to break out of the mold.

And down the years, should you see a young lady on television by the name of Rhonda Spiller who wins a gold medal as a gymnast, remember where she got her start: On the second pew in the middle section of the Tinyburg Church!

A Sunday in Bigtown

Although Candice Spiller attended college only a year, she and her roommate, Beverly, became lifetime friends. Beverly married a successful architect in Bigtown. Beverly named her first baby Bruce, and Candice called hers Rhonda.

The two families kept in close touch, visiting back and forth. The summer that Bruce was ten and Rhonda was eight, the Spillers invited Bruce to Tinyburg for a week. Bruce, a precocious youngster in an accelerated program at school, balked at visiting an eight-year-old girl in a town of only 1,473 residents.

"You'll be surprised at all the good times you can have in a small town," his daddy said. "In turn, Rhonda can visit us here in Bigtown."

The first day or two in Tinyburg, Bruce was bored. But on Wednesday, Rhonda's grandpa, Clay Barker, invited Rhonda and Bruce to an old-time farm auction.

"What's an auction?" wondered Bruce, as Rhonda explained: "Oh, it's where a family sells everything out on the front lawn, and my Grandpa, the auctioneer, says funny words no one understands, and people hold up their hands, and he cries 'Sold' so loud your ears pop."

Bruce was impressed with the long string of pickup trucks parked on both sides of a lane leading to the farm. Also he wondered why Mr. Barker wore his coat and tie all day, even though the perspiration ran down his face and dripped off his chin.

"Son, in my business, where you're dealing with the public, buying and selling, you demand respect by the way you dress.

I'd no more go out to sell a piece of property in my shirt sleeves than I'd be buried in a clown suit!"

Best of all, Bruce devoured the homemade ham sandwiches and soft drinks which a ladies' group sold from a concession stand. And it was fun, watching the buyers round up the livestock, pigs, or chickens they bought, then load their trucks with antique furniture, old farm tools, homemade quilts, dishes and glassware, and a thousand other strange-looking items—strange, that is, to a city boy.

Although Bruce didn't need a haircut, he got a kick out of going to the Purple Crackerbox with Ted Spiller, Rhonda's daddy. The Purple Crackerbox is what George Mason named his barbershop.

"When I bought this one-room building and converted it into a barbershop, everyone laughed at the bright purple paint the former owner used on the concrete blocks," he explained to Bruce. "So I just capitalized on the joke by calling it The Purple Crackerbox. Some of the best advertising I ever did. Draws customers from miles around." And although Bruce had a fresh haircut when he arrived in Tinyburg, he wasn't satisfied until he sat in George's barber chair for a trim.

"You're lucky you came this week," announced Candice the next morning as she fixed waffles and strawberries for Bruce and Rhonda's breakfast. "Tonight we're surprising a widower in our church, William Cutrell, on his eightieth birthday. Or Uncle Billy Told-You-So, as he's known. Only we're calling it a baby shower, so he won't get suspicious."

Bruce had fun that night sitting in the darkened church basement with about a hundred guests as they waited to sing "Happy Birthday" when Uncle Billy stumbled in, supposedly to replace a burned-out light fuse. He remembers the old-time singalong featuring "I've Been Workin' on the Railroad," "Let Me Call You Sweetheart," and "Down by the Old Mill Stream."

Best of all, he liked the homemade ice cream served on the church lawn, under a string of Japanese lanterns.

On Sunday, the Spillers took Bruce to church and introduced him to the Preacher. "You mean you're the minister?" Bruce replied. "I go to the Bigtown Church. I bet you know our minister—the Reverend Doctor Henry Moss?"

"Yes, I know Henry," replied the Preacher. "But do you call him by that fancy title?"

"We have to," replied Bruce. "He says it shows proper respect."

As Bruce sat near the front with the Spillers, he saw an older woman come in with a bouquet for the communion table. Only the flowers were in a Maxwell House coffee can! "Can't your church afford a vase?" Bruce whispered to Rhonda. "Oh, that's Pearl Ramsey—moved here from the country. She's used to bringing flowers in coffee cans, so my grandmother, who's the flower chairman, told her it's okay."

In the middle of the song service, the director asked if "anyone's got a favorite you'd like to sing?" All around, worshipers called out page numbers in the hymnal. This puzzled Bruce, for he thought the song director was talking about favorite movies or baseball players.

At the dinner table, Ted Spiller asked Bruce how he liked their church. "It's not like ours in Bigtown. Your choir doesn't even wear robes. And there was so much talking before the service. At home, everybody sits quiet, like a funeral. You don't even sneeze, honest, no matter how bad you want to."

A few weeks later, it was Rhonda's turn to visit Bigtown. It was so exciting, being in a real city! One day she went with Bruce to his day camp, and another day to the country club, where she must have climbed five hundred trips up the big sliding board that landed you in the swimming pool. They went to movies, to an amusement park, the zoo, and joined a cookout in a neighbor's backyard.

Then on Sunday, to the Bigtown Church. The ushers wore white matching jackets with tiny red rosebuds in the lapels. And the carpet was so deep and soft it was like walking on a fresh patch of clover back in Tinyburg. The choir wore dark blue robes; soft candles glowed on the altar; and a huge floral arrangement filled a massive brass bowl on the communion table.

No one whispered or looked around at anyone. She worried she might sneeze or cough. The organist, seated at the biggest pipe organ Rhonda had ever seen, played solemn music that made her feel as if she were at a funeral.

Then came the processional, consisting of the pastor's staff, a dozen deacons, and the choir singing, "Holy, holy, holy, Lord God Almighty. . . ."

Once the choir, deacons, and staff reached their assigned seats, the minister, wearing a clerical gown trimmed in red velvet, entered and made his way up the three steps to the pulpit. At the exact moment the Reverend Doctor Henry Moss reached the third step, the entire congregation, out of long habit, stood in respect as if executing a military drill. And by now the choir was singing "Cherubim and seraphim falling down before thee!" Plus a long choral Amen.

As the music faded, and while the people were still standing, Reverend Moss read in the most dignified voice you can imagine:

> In the year that King Uzziah died I saw also the Lord sitting upon a throne, high and lifted up, and his train filled the temple. Above it stood the seraphims: each one had six wings: with twain he covered his face, and with twain he covered his feet, and with twain he did fly. And one cried unto another, and said, Holy, holy, holy, is the Lord of hosts: the whole earth is full of his glory. And the posts of the door moved at the voice of him that cried, and the house was filled with smoke (Isa. 6:1-4).

At this point, overwhelmed by the grandeur of it all, little Rhonda tugged at the sleeve of Bruce's mother and whispered,

"Beverly, does your minister live here all week, or just come down from heaven on Sundays?"

The next Sunday, back in Tinyburg, the Preacher greeted Rhonda warmly and asked if she'd had fun in Bigtown. Ignoring his question, she looked him in the eyes as trusting as only an eight-year-old can and said, "I like you Preacher, because you live here all week!"

"Why, where else could I live?"

Then she described the gilt and glitter of the Bigtown Church, and how glad she was to be home with her friends.

The Preacher laughed, good-naturedly, as if to reassure Rhonda that all's well in Tinyburg. Then he explained, in language a little girl understands:

"Rhonda, we read in the Old Testament how God's people first worshiped in a tabernacle, a sort of portable tent. Later, when they could afford better, they erected a magnificent Temple in Jerusalem of the best materials, such as stone, cedar, gold, silver, and brass. Later, when the Jewish people were scattered in war, they met in simple synagogues. And after Jesus came, the Christians met in what we'd call housechurches. Eventually they built churches of their own, some of them masterpieces, such as the great cathedrals of Europe and England.

"But what we must understand, Rhonda, is that some people like big churches, and some like little churches. At times, Christians have met in the open air, under trees, or in makeshift brush arbors. Some prefer anthems, others enjoy gospel songs. But what matters is feeling God in our hearts."

Then he reached in his notebook and tore out a little poem: "Take this home and ask your Daddy to read it, maybe at the dinner table."

Here's what it said:

> Beautiful is the large church,
> With stately arch and steeple;
> Neighborly is the small church,

With groups of friendly people;
Reverent is the old church,
With centuries of grace;
And a wooden church or a stone church
Can hold an altar place.
And whether it be a rich church
Or a poor church anyplace,
Truly it is a great church
If God is worshiped there.

I hope you'll visit the Tinyburg Church, and when you do, I trust you feel God's presence.

One thing I do know—the Preacher lives in Tinyburg all week!

A Wedding at Willow Creek

About an hour's drive west of Tinyburg, and just over the county line, is Willow Creek State Park, its gently flowing streams feeding into a big lake, noted for its fishing and water skiing. The park boasts a rustic lodge with a massive dining room overlooking the lake, as well as hiking and bicycle paths, swimming pool, and golf course. Also a natural amphitheater with 2,000 seats, a popular place for outdoor musicals as well as an annual Easter sunrise service.

All the time their children were growing up, Willow Creek Park was a favorite for picnicking and camping by Ted and Candice Spiller. And when Rhonda, their oldest, fell in love with Jack Easley in Bigtown, she dreamed of an outdoor wedding in the park.

"Surely not in that big amphitheater?" questioned Candice. "We'd be lost in that monstrosity. Besides, think of all the trouble in an outdoor wedding. And what if it rains?"

Rhonda reminded her parents that when they were married in the Tinyburg Church twenty-five years ago, they had caused all kinds of commotion by insisting the Sunday School curtains be taken down, upsetting the whole congregation the following Sunday. At the time, the curtains crisscrossed the church sanctuary, suspended on sturdy clothesline wires and anchored securely, like a battleship, with turnbuckles in the wall.

So they agreed on an outdoor ceremony and Candice and Ted announced the wedding for sunset on Friday, May 31. A wedding dinner in the lodge would follow for the sixty invited guests. Also, Jack and Rhonda had reserved the honeymoon suite in the lodge for the weekend.

"Mother," Rhonda beamed, "such an easy wedding to get ready for—no candles or flowers for the church, no lost motion getting to the reception and honeymoon. And all in a beautiful, romantic setting!"

"I hope so," her daddy agreed, recalling other "simple" plans that had gone awry in the Barker-Spiller families. He remembered how he broke his wrist on his own wedding day, over twenty-five years ago. That morning, in a hurry to buy travelers' checks at the Tinyburg National Bank, he had walked right through a set of new glass doors.

May 31 was a bride's dream. Scattered white puffs of clouds dotted an otherwise clear, brilliant blue sky. And by sunset, the wedding in the park took on a picture-book setting.

Rhonda persuaded her grandpa, Clay Barker, to wear a dressy handkerchief in his breast coat pocket, instead of his usual array of gaily colored felt-tip and ball-point pens. As president of the Tinyburg Realty Company, Clay goes nowhere without a ready supply of pens. "Never know when you'll find a chance to close a deal," he explains. "But Grandpa, you're not going to sell farms and houses at my wedding," Rhonda argued, winning the day.

Aunt Sarah Biggs, one of the guests, said she always wondered what a Hollywood set looked like, and now she knew. It was breathtaking! The Preacher wrote a special ceremony for the occasion, quoting from the second chapter of the Song of Solomon:

> My beloved, . . . said unto me, Rise up, my love, my fair one, and come away. For, lo, the winter is past, the rain is over and gone; The flowers appear on the earth, the time of the singing of birds is come, and the voice of the turtle is heard in our land (vv. 10-13).

Aunt Sarah, who keeps oodles of scrapbooks filled with newspaper clippings, snapshots, and locks of baby hair, liked the poetry the Preacher quoted in the ceremony. He gladly gave her copies which occupy an honored place in one of her scrapbooks. She arranged the poetry on the same page where she mounted a pressed rosebud from Rhonda's bridal bouquet.

Helen Keller, who at the age of nineteen months was left blind and deaf by a crippling illness, was the author of the first poem:

> In merry mood I leave the crowd
> To walk in my garden. Ever as I walk
> I gather fruits and flowers in my hands.
> And with joyful heart I bless the sun
> That kindles all the place with radiant life.
>
> I run with playful winds that blow the scent
> Of rose and jessamine in eddying whirls.
> At last I come where tall lilies grow,
> Lifting their faces like white saints to God.
> While the lilies pray, I kneel upon the ground;
> I have strayed into the holy temple of the Lord.

The second piece Aunt Sarah saved in her scrapbook is stanza four of "God's Garden" by Dorothy F. Gurney (1858-1932). It's the same stanza inscribed at the Bok Singing Tower in Lake Wales, Florida:

> The kiss of the sun for pardon,
>   The song of the birds for mirth,—
> One is nearer God's heart in a garden
>   Than anywhere else on earth.

For the benediction, the Preacher asked God to bless the marriage with the softness of an evening in May, and with children as beautiful as a June morning.

By the time the wedding supper ended and the Preacher and his wife, Carol, had driven back to Tinyburg, it was a quarter 'til midnight. "Think I'll sit up a few minutes and finish signing Rhonda and Jack's wedding papers," he told Carol. "I should mail the license back to the county clerk first thing in the morning."

Carol was barely in bed when the Preacher screamed, "That couple's not married!"

"How can you say that when we just came home from the wedding? You performed the ceremony yourself! Somebody put the wrong thing in your punch, you talking that way."

"Don't kid me," the Preacher replied soberly. "This marriage license plainly reads, 'Good only in Bluford County.' That's where we live. But Willow Creek State Park is five miles across the line, in the next county. Poor little Rhonda and Jack—living in sin—don't realize what they're doing—and it's my fault for not telling them to get their license in that county. This calls for action. Quick, back the car out of the garage while I get them on the phone."

The desk clerk argued that it was unusual to ring the honeymoon suite after midnight, except in an emergency. "This *is* an emergency!" the Preacher shot back. "Besides, I'm their pastor." Thinking it must be a death message or something, the clerk quickly put his call through.

"Hello, hello, Jack! That you? Say, have you gone to bed yet?"

"What do you mean have I gone to bed yet? Is this April Fools' Day? If so, find someone else to play your cheap jokes on!"

"Joke or no joke, don't go to bed until I get there," the Preacher replied. "You could be living in adultery. Son, you're not married yet!"

Still thinking he was the victim of a crude prankster, Jack was ready to slam the receiver down when the Preacher convinced him he was serious. "You and Rhonda get dressed, meet me in the lobby. I'll drive as fast as I can and be there about 1 AM. Then we'll come back in my car, just across the county line, where I'll tie the knot so good that even the Supreme Court can't find a loophole."

The Preacher burned up the highway to the Willow Creek Lodge, arriving about 12:45 AM. It was now Saturday morning, June 1. The three lost no time backtracking the five miles to Bluford County. Once safely across the line, the Preacher pulled off to the side of the road and performed the shortest wedding in the state's history. It consisted of exactly eleven words. Here they are: "Do you kids want to get married? Yes. Then you're married!" Rhonda braced herself for a long benediction, but the Preacher skipped the formalities.

Back home, he scrambled some eggs to settle his nerves, then completed the license, changing the date of the ceremony from May 31 to June 1. The *Tinyburg News* dutifully reported that Rhonda Spiller and Jack Easley were married in a quiet but scenic lakeside ceremony at sundown on Friday, May 31. But the records in the courthouse say it was Saturday, June 1, in Bluford County.

A year or so later Rhonda gave birth to twins—dainty little girls whom she and Jack named May and June. When June, the more precocious of the sisters, was about five, she asked if having twins had anything to do with getting married twice on the same day. Jack, who thought the question was hilarious, said, if so, he was grateful they weren't married three times, or else triplets would be underfoot. And although the twins didn't quite understand, Rhonda went on to explain that Mommy and Daddy were married once to honor God, and once to please the laws of Bluford County.

One aspect of the double wedding continues to bless the Easley home. Each year, they observe two anniversaries, sort of a "his" and "hers." On May 31 Rhonda and Jack treat themselves to a private celebration. On June 1 they take off another day, making it a family treat. And the Preacher, for fun, sends them two anniversary cards, one for May 31 and one for June 1. The first card is comic, while the second is serious and sentimental.

Oh, one other thing. The Preacher has never forgotten where the county line is!

If you ever vacation at Willow Creek State Park, stop at the Tinyburg Cafe, either going or coming. In case no one has told you, it's the home of the world-famous Tinyburger, where you always get two for the price of one.

Over the Hill

Minutes after the morning mail arrived, Candice Spiller called her mother, Mrs. Clay Barker: "Mom, don't fix that birthday dinner for me and my family this evening. We can't come."

"What do you mean you can't come? Half the dinner's cooked and I baked your favorite coconut layer cake yesterday. All it lacks is the frosting."

"But Mom, you don't understand. I just can't make it. I can't."

"Candice, whatever's gotten into you?" her mother replied, half scolding. "The only time in forty years we've not been together on your birthday was the year you went away to college. Even when you were in bed with the measles, when you were five, I painted faces on balloons and dotted their little cheeks to look like they had the measles, too."

"If I were five years old again, Mom, I'd run to your house. But I'm not five. I'm forty and I can't accept it. And if you'd see the card from one of my so-called friends, you'd know what I mean. It's supposed to be funny, but it's not funny to me. Edged in black to look like a sympathy card. It reads, 'Sorry you're over the hill—see you at the bottom.' And the artwork's a tombstone."

"Candice, everybody jokes about fortieth birthdays. Your friend meant no harm. You can't take things like that personally."

"Mom, it may be a joke to some, but not to me. I was already blue, and then came that card like a torpedo and sank what little joy I had. I'm taking two aspirins and going back to bed. When Carl gets home, he and I can go to the drive-in, then to a movie. But I don't want any cake and certainly no party."

By now, Mrs. Barker's tone of voice turned from half-scold to full-scold: "Candice, I'm putting on my walking shoes and you put on yours, too. I'll be by in five minutes."

But the harshness melted into motherly love and compassion when Mrs. Barker walked in and saw the red-lined eyes of her forty-year-old daughter. She took her in her arms as if she were a little girl again and, between sobs, whispered, "I know how you feel, Candice. I was there myself, not too long ago."

Then wiping her eyes, she regained some of her sternness as she ordered, "On with those comfortable old shoes you wear in the garden—you and I are going for a long walk in the country."

It was the kind of fall day that makes the countryside around Tinyburg look, each October, like a giant painting. There had been one light frost and two heavy ones. The bright sunlight glistened on the red and yellow and brown foliage of the trees, while red sumac, goldenrod, and purple asters formed a stunning backdrop.

They walked west of town for about three miles, until the little country church of Ebenezer came in view. Across the road from the church, on a gentle hillside, was an old cemetery, some of it abandoned, the grave markers ancient and tottering.

At the cemetery, Mrs. Barker made as if she would open the rusty gate to go inside. "No, Mom," Candice drew back. "All I can see is that horrible birthday card about being over the hill."

"I want to help, not hurt you," Mrs. Barker replied gently, as she nudged her into the cemetery. "Look how many little markers there are for babies and children. You see them in all the older cemeteries. There was a time when many babies died at birth, or just a year or two old.

"In newer cemeteries, you don't see nearly as many baby graves in proportion to the others. Before the days of antibiotics and vaccines, so many little ones died of whooping cough, diphtheria, smallpox, and the like. Poor things, they never had a chance.

"Here's a tiny marker that reads, 'Baby Joe, 1 month, 13 days.' And another, 'Asleep in Jesus, age one year.' And that one over there, 'Infant angel, June 21, 1883—June 22, 1883.' Lived only a day.'"

Throughout the cemetery, Mrs. Barker pointed to similar markers, as well as those of mothers who died in their twenties, of youngsters who passed away at age eight, or eleven, or fifteen.

Then turning to Candice, she said, "You're probably wondering why I brought you here. Yes, I have a reason. I want to remind you how fortunate we are to have lived as long as we have. Whenever we dread birthdays and get depressed over growing old, we're really saying, 'I regret I've lived this long.' But Candice, is that what we mean to say?

"If you're unhappy to be forty (and I'm not jumping up and down myself about being sixty-eight), does that mean we'd like to change places with these mothers and their little ones who lived so briefly?

"Let's face it—if one of these youngsters could listen in, would we want him to hear us say we're sorry to be as old as we are? He might well say, 'I wish I'd had a chance to live to be half your age.'

"I'm thinking now of Opal and Earl Baggett, who lost one of their sons in the war. Stepped on a land mine and never knew what hit him. Brought him home in a bronze casket, flag and honor guard and all that. Opal later told me there wasn't a cup full of black dirt in that casket—she and Earl regretted they ever brought him back.

"He was barely nineteen. Never knew what it was to be a

father, to run and play with his own little ones. He'd be envious of you and all the other forty-year-olds, for you've already lived twice as long."

Candice gripped her mother's hand. "Mom, you're right. It's just that everybody makes so much over getting old, and joking you, and all that."

"I know what you mean. Maybe those who can't accept their age are the ones who joke the loudest. They laugh, out of fear they might cry."

On their way back to Tinyburg, Mrs. Barker picked up the conversation:

"Yesterday when I was baking your cake and wondering if it was big enough to hold forty candles, I splattered a big tear in the cake mix. Nothing makes a mother feel older than to see her children reach forty and beyond.

"Then I decided we appreciate most what we have less of. And as we age, we have fewer years. I remember my own mother who kept a big cookie bowl in the middle of our farm kitchen table. If she didn't have time to bake a pie or cake for dinner, she'd say, 'Just finish off with a cookie or two.' And when I came home from school, hungry for a snack, she said, 'Look in the cookie bowl!'

"Saturday was her day for baking cookies, enough to last all week. Sugar cookies, oatmeal cookies, cinnamon cookies, lemon cookies, black walnut cookies—she was an expert in all of them. By Thursday or Friday, the cookie bowl would be running low. And you know, the nearer we reached the bottom, the better they tasted, even if some were broken and crumbly. Then at the last, say on Friday night, we rationed them among ourselves.

"So Candice, as we grow older, aware that the years are slipping by, we make the special days stand out more than ever. Every birthday must be a *precious* birthday—one without tears, but with gratitude we've lived as long as we have. The same with other festive occasions—Easter, Thanksgiving, Christmas, wedding anniversaries. . . .

"And when some thoughtless persons say we're over the hill, it's time for us to say that if we have reached the summit, this means a lot of rough and slippery places are behind us. We've made it! Hallelujah! Maybe going down won't be as hard as coming up."

"Mother, you're a jewel," Candice said as she hugged her again, back at the house. "How can I ever pay you back?"

"Easy," said her mother. "Someday, when I'm gone, tell your kids what I've told you today."

With a little imagination, you can appreciate that the fortieth birthday party that night was one of the most festive in the history of the Barker family. They *still* talk about it.

Following an old custom, members of the Tinyburg Church give birthday offerings based on their age. Children usually give a penny a year, and adults drop in a quarter or so for each year.

On the next Sunday, after Candice dropped in forty quarters and the members sang, "Happy Birthday," someone whispered, "Candice, I thought you were thirty-nine and holding."

"No," she replied. "I'm forty and turning loose!"

Everything But the Baby

Edith and Clay Barker were ecstatic when their daughter, Kay, announced she'd have a baby in July.

"Imagine, you and me a grandpa and grandma," Edith said to Clay after the momentous call from San Diego, where Kay and her husband, Ron, live. "I can't believe it. Oh, I wish they lived closer. We'll never get to see the little fellow."

"Fellow?" asked Clay. "How do you know it'll be a boy?"

"Whatever it is. You know as busy as Ron is, they won't come home any oftener with a baby than they have in the six years they've been married. You can count on the fingers of one hand the nights that Ron Bouton has slept in this house."

True, Ron and Kay were caught up in their own life-style in San Diego. Ron came from a well-to-do family in Boston, attended parochial schools, then an ivy league college where he earned a degree in engineering. A job in San Diego with a big electronics firm was waiting, even before he graduated. Ron, a Catholic, had grown up in a big church, a parish of 1,600 families.

The first time Kay brought her fiancee home to Tinyburg, she introduced him to Uncle Billy Cutrell as "Mr. Bouton."

"Is that pronounced baton, like a band director uses, or booton, like you say 'boo' to scare a baby?" he inquired, innocently. Kay was incensed: "Mother, Uncle Billy embarrassed me to pieces at church—asked if my Ron's name was like saying 'boo' to a baby."

"He meant no harm. Uncle Billy's a friendly person who likes to know people."

"In my opinion, some things are better unsaid," Kay retorted.

When July rolled around and the birth announcement came from San Diego in a midnight phone call, Edith and Clay never went back to bed. They kept saying to each other, "Kay has a baby boy! We're grandparents of a future president!"

The next few months produced a flurry of calls to and from San Diego, and about once a week a postman delivered another packet of color photos. By October, Edith began her third album of pictures of Ron, Jr. It was Ron, Jr. laughing at the camera, Ron, Jr. tasting his first ice cream, Ron, Jr.'s first day at the beach, and on and on. Candice, the Barker's younger daughter, said that if she had a baby, there'd be no film left in the stores—her sister had bought every roll for Ron, Jr.

The Barkers set the following summer to drive out to San Diego. By then, Ron, Jr. would be walking. Then at Thanksgiving, Kay called, saying she and Ron were coming for Christmas: "Ron's never been in Tinyburg during the holidays, and it will be fun to celebrate the baby's first Christmas together. We'll fly to Bigtown, then drive a rental car to Tinyburg. Ron doesn't mind the expense, so forget about meeting us."

Edith had mixed feelings about the Christmas visit. She couldn't wait to see her first grandchild. On the other hand, she didn't know Ron well enough to feel relaxed around him. His background was so different—reared in a big city, used to plenty of money. Would he enjoy her cooking? Feel at home in a small town, attending a little church?

"Edith, he puts his pants on like any other man," Clay said, trying to bolster her courage. "You'll be so busy with Ron, Jr. you won't have time to worry whether he likes the way you roast a turkey."

"I hope you're right," Edith said, with lingering apprehension.

About the middle of December, Clay complained their house was beginning to look like an army surplus store. "Edith, we're not feeding an army," he half scolded. "And all these blankets and heating pads and bottle warmers and diapers. They'll only be here four days, not four months."

"Being a man, you don't understand," Edith said. "Ron and Kay aren't used to cold weather. Neither is the baby. Who knows, a blizzard might close the stores, and us with no food or baby supplies. It could be a disaster. And yes, maybe I did splurge on decorations and gifts. But Clay, this Christmas is different. There'll never be another like it—with our first grandchild."

"It *will* be different!" he agreed.

Although Edith and Clay could hardly keep from driving to the airport, they waited patiently until Ron, Kay, and the baby pulled into the driveway in a rental car. Only it wasn't a car—it was the biggest station wagon they'd seen.

Once the hugging and kissing and oohing and aahing were over, Clay raised the question about why such a big station wagon. Ron answered: "Kay said we'd best prepare for bad weather, maybe the stores closing, so we brought extra supplies, you know, blankets and diapers and bottle warmers. And so he'd feel at home, we threw in Ron, Jr.'s playthings."

By the time Clay helped unload the station wagon, he decided their house looked like two army surplus stores.

Christmas Eve fell on a Sunday, and the Barkers were up long before daylight so everyone could be on time for Sunday School. For most of their friends at church, it would be their first opportunity to see little Ron, Jr.

"Mother, I think we'd better take two cars," Kay suggested about an hour before church time. "I want plenty of blankets and diapers. The nursery might be cold."

Clay noted: "Kay, the first time we took you to church, your mother and I walked and carried you and one small diaper bag. And now you're taking two car loads of people and supplies for little Ron, Jr. By the time you have a grandkid of your own, you'll need a U-haul truck."

"Clay," interrupted Edith, "let's mind our own business and let them take what they want. Little Ron, Jr. is used to warm weather in San Diego, and I wouldn't want him to get sick because of an argument over taking one car or two cars."

Edith and Clay left a few minutes ahead of Ron and Kay. "The baby will be fine in the nursery, and we'll sit together during the church service," Edith called to Kay through the bathroom door.

Mrs. Barker was about 15 minutes into teaching her ladies Bible class when Opal Baggett walked in. Edith paused to ask if Opal saw her new grandson.

"Stopped by the nursery, but he wasn't in there," Opal replied.

"What do you mean he wasn't in there? Of course he is—we spent half a day getting everyone ready for Sunday School."

"That's what I thought. But I didn't see any baby that looked like Kay's. And I think I know every tyke in Tinyburg."

Although upset that Opal couldn't pick out the prettiest baby that ever laid in a crib in the Tinyburg Church, Edith continued with the lesson. However, her mind on the baby, she voiced her misgivings: "Excuse me, ladies. I'm going across the hall to peek in the nursery. Maybe Ron couldn't start the station wagon."

At the nursery door a helper said she hadn't seen the baby: "Yes, I saw Kay and Ron get out of their car, but they weren't carrying a baby."

By now Edith was wondering if, like Scrooge, she was having a bad Christmas dream. Running to Kay's classroom, she motioned her out in the hall. "Where's little Ron, Jr.?" Edith asked, trying to keep calm.

"Mother, what do you mean where's little Ron? You and Dad brought him to church yourselves!"

"Brought him to church?" screamed Edith, her voice pitched high with anxiety. "We thought you did! Kay, you mean that precious little darling baby boy's at home by himself, and him only six months old?"

Speechless, Kay fumbled in her purse for her car keys and

ran to the parking lot. "Hurry, Kay, you know I've always been afraid of fire. I could have left the oven on . . . the house full of smoke, maybe. . . ."

Clay, alarmed by the commotion outside his classroom, opened the door just in time to hear the words fire, smoke, and baby. Wasting no time, he ran to the church office: "Call the fire department; call the rescue squad; call the Tinyburg police; call the state police! Our house is afire . . . little Ron trapped inside!"

Within minutes, everyone heard the wail of sirens and as the news spread from class to class, a sort of pre-Christmas pandemonium set in.

Then someone cried, "Here comes a police car, its blue light spinning round and round." Sure enough, down the street came a police car leading a station wagon, with Kay at the wheel. A slight warming trend about sunup had blanketed Tinyburg with a thick, winter fog, and the lights of the police car made an eerie sight as it pulled up to the front of the church.

Breathlessly, Edith, Clay, and the baby's daddy rushed to the station wagon and reached inside for Ron, Jr.

"Oh, my precious little Christmas baby," Edith wailed, "did that fire scare you? Kay, did he breathe any smoke?"

Kay, the only calm person in the congregation, which now lined the steps and sidewalk, laughed: "Mother, there wasn't any fire. We got our signals mixed. Little Ron was sleeping peacefully. His daddy and I thought you were bringing him. And you thought we were. We were so preoccupied with his bottles and blankets that we forgot the baby!"

There was nothing to do but dismiss Sunday School, for no one's mind was on the lesson. So everyone visited and introduced themselves to Ron, Sr. and patted the baby until you would have thought folks in Tinyburg had never seen a six-month baby. Truth is, this *was* their first time to see a baby of any age chauffered to church by a police car.

During the worship service, Uncle Billy Cutrell beckoned to the Preacher and asked if he could make a special announcement.

Making his way slowly to the front, he began, "Folks, I've lost track of how many Christmases I've celebrated in the Tinyburg Church. Lots of good ones, a few bad ones, due to illness or hard times or the Grim Reaper. But never a Christmas like today. When I stood outside, scared we might never see Clay's grandbaby alive, I watched this revolving blue light, coming through the fog. As it drew closer, you could tell it was a police car, and then you saw the station wagon, and then that tiny brown-headed baby peeking out of his little blue blanket. I could have shouted, but I was too choked up.

"Then while listening to Laura Jane play the prelude, 'It Came upon the Midnight Clear,' I thought of another revolving light, centuries ago, which they called a star. The world was cold and the night dark, but that star shone so brightly that Wise Men followed it hundreds of miles to the Christ child in Bethlehem.

"Each Christmas, we work ourselves into a frenzy over what we'll give and get, worried about this and that. And in so doing, we miss the real meaning of Christmas, which is a baby.

"Oh, I don't mean my good friends the Barkers and the Batons—that is, the Bootons, or whichever it is—I don't mean they forgot their grandbaby intentionally. Any of us could have done the same, with so much to look after. I use them as a reminder of what happens every Christmas, only in different ways."

The audience was visibly moved. After Uncle Billy sat down, the Preacher added, "Folks, you've just heard all the sermon you'll hear today. What I prepared can wait—maybe until next Christmas. We have the baby. We have each other. And that's all that matters."

Through the years, Kay and Ron have continued to visit Tinyburg. They still bring two or three times as much luggage as they need, even since their family grew to three children. And Edith still cooks more than anyone can eat, and Clay buys more toys than they could ever wear out.

But never, never, never, have they lost a baby. Or each other!

"See You in the Funny Papers!"

One of the slowest moving persons in Tinyburg is a young man in his early thirties by the name of Jimmie Swan. Jimmie, who's a dishwasher at the Tinyburg Nursing Home, sort of shuffles along. "Jimmie, when Gabriel blows his horn, you'll never make it inside the Pearly Gates, unless I'm there to give you a hand," is how Aunt Sarah Biggs scolds him, good-naturedly.

Jimmie is invariably late for church. But regardless of who's sitting where, he insists on coming down to the second pew from the front, in the middle section. Whoever's next to the aisle, he climbs over to reach the exact center of the middle pew.

"Don't feel as if I've been to church unless I can look the Preacher right in the eye," is how he puts it.

Jimmie Swan may be slow, but there's one thing he can do better and quicker than anyone in Tinyburg. And that's the talent of making people laugh. You might say he's a Peter Pan kind of a fellow, who never wants to grow up.

Not that he's childish—but he just lives by the philosophy that a little fun along the way sort of lubricates the rough spots. He likes to mimic Mary Poppins by humming the tune about a spoonful of sugar making "the medicine go down."

His by-word is, "I'll see you in the funny paper!" It's an old saying he picked up from an uncle, back when folks referred to the Sunday comics as the "funny papers."

Jimmie never thought of himself as a celebrity and that's why he was surprised back in 1982 when the city council voted him "Man of the Year of Tinyburg."

"Why I've never held any public office, don't even have a

107

white-collar job," he apologized, when the mayor called to announce the award.

"Jimmie, you've got one talent that makes up for everything," the mayor replied. "You know how to make people laugh. I don't know where you learned it."

"I sure didn't learn it at no clown school," Jimmie laughed. "Fact is, I didn't graduate from high school. Just started working, odd jobs here and there."

"Were you always a cutup, back as a boy?" the mayor continued.

"No, sir—I started this fun thing once I got this job at the nursing home," he replied. "I saw so many older patients, sitting there day after day, never smiling, never chuckling, never laughing. Oh, we saw to it that they had warm, nourishing food and proper medical care.

"But folks in the sunset years deserve to laugh and enjoy themselves, as well as youngsters in the sunrise years. I figured our patients had had their share of pain and sorrow in life. Why not help them feel like kids again? And I learned that if I made them feel like a kid again, I'd have to act that way myself, at least once in a while.

"So what I do is play the fool every chance I get. Then I tell my experiences to the patients. They enjoy hearing about my shennanigans as much as I do putting them on."

Jimmie received his "Man of the Year" award at a recognition dinner, attended by 125 townspeople. For the program, the mayor asked four persons to tell some far-out examples of Jimmie's humor.

The first speaker was Burt David:

"I'd just moved here and didn't know anyone, when I stopped at the Tinyburg Cafe for lunch.

"This young fellow, who I later learned was Jimmie, came in with a quart thermos bottle and a small ice chest. He went from table to table, asking customers that if any coffee was left in their cups, could he pour it in his thermos.

"He came over to my table, but I was drinking iced tea. So he had the nerve to ask for the leftover ice in the bottom of my glass, which he dumped in his ice chest.

"My first thought was that here's some idiot boy who needs to be in an institution. When I asked what he wanted with the ice, he said the refrigerators at the Tinyburg Nursing Home needed repairs and they were out of ice. Also said one of the patients drinks thirty cups of coffee a day, and they can't afford that much coffee. So Jimmie bums off the community.

"Honest, Jimmie wore such a straight face, I thought maybe he was for real. I also wondered if Tinyburg were some sort of haven for oddballs, sort of a dumping ground for the characters in Ripley's 'Believe-It-Or-Not.'

"Later I learned that he regaled the patients with fits of laughter when he got back and reported on how much ice he'd collected, how people looked when he begged them for leftover coffee, and the like.

"'Course they didn't heat up that coffee and drink it, but I learned one patient who'd been a bookkeeper keeps a weekly tally of how many pounds of ice and how many gallons of coffee that Jimmie collects off newcomers to the cafe!

"'Beats watchin' those television game shows all day,'" he told his roommate at the home.

The second speaker was the Preacher's eleven-year-old son, Mark:

"I was selling magazine subscriptions, calling prospects on the telephone. And when I got Jimmie on the phone, he started asking all these funny questions.

"He first asked me how much my magazines weighed and I asked him what difference that makes. He said if you buy bananas or hamburger, you want to know how many pounds. So he made me go and weigh a sample magazine and report the number of ounces. Then he sent me back to divide the number of pages into the number of ounces, to get the average weight of each page. He was really getting into tough math!

"Next, he wanted to know how much a subscription is by the ounce if you divide the price by the number of pounds in all the issues for one year. So I said, 'Jimmie, you don't need magazines, you need a home computer, and hung up on him.'

"Later, he did buy a subscription, but not before he involved the patients in deciding which magazine to buy, based, believe it or not, on the cost per ounce. No one but Jimmie Swan would buy magazines on that basis. Maybe we should name him 'Man of the Century' as well."

The third speaker was Mrs. Clay Barker, who described a potluck supper at the church:

"Here came Jimmie with a bean pot, but no food. When I asked why, he acted as if he didn't know you're supposed to bring food to a potluck supper. I asked if he thought we'd eat our imaginations. He said no, but that a potluck means a 'pot of luck.' So he'd brought good luck pieces in his pot, but no food.

"Naturally, we let him eat, but not until he'd explained the contents of his pot. He first brought out a horseshoe, saying every sensible farmer nails one over his barn door for good luck. Then he fished around and brought out six tiny four-leaf clovers. Said the patients helped him find them. He reminded us what we've always known, that four-leaf clovers mean good luck.

"Next he brought out a small bag of navy beans, saying every housewife knows that if she serves beans on New Year's Day, her family will enjoy prosperity for the next twelve months. The last item in the bean pot was a live butterfly, its little wings still fluttering. He said this was his favorite good-luck charm, for when a butterfly lights on a little girl, it's a sign she'll get a new dress the color of its wings. He then turned it loose, and every woman present tried to attract the butterfly's attention, but it flew out a window. He said the patients came up with the idea, and some of them had fun chasing butterflies with nets on the lawn.

"Jimmie ended by joking that the manager of the Nursing Home had promised him a new job, that of recreation director."

The last speaker at the awards dinner was a gangling teenager by the name of Cecil, who'd just bought his first car:

"I was answering a want ad for a used car, but I dialed a wrong number and got Jimmie.

"Although Jimmie's never owned a car of any kind, he played me along, making me think he'd placed the ad.

"When I said I was answering his ad, he asked if I wanted a good model car, and I said yes, that's why I was calling. He then asked what model I wanted and I said I preferred a hatchback Honda. And he said that's what he had, but what year did I have in mind, and I said 1979. And he said that's a coincidence, for he had it.

"When I asked what color it was, he asked what color I wanted and I said a dark brown with white stripes, and he said that's what he had. By now I should have caught on, but I guess I was naive. When I asked how much he wanted, he asked how much I wanted to pay. And I said no more than I had to. And he said he didn't want to sell it for any more than he had to.

"By now, I was wondering whether I had dialed a clown, or maybe this was just my lucky day. So I asked him where I could see the Honda, and he said there in his apartment. I thought he meant parked on the street. He said no, right there on a shelf in his bedroom. I guess I thought he meant a garage attached to the house, so I walked over to see it.

"When I got there, I learned he collects model cars—all kinds. Shelves of them. And there was my 1979 Honda hatchback, dark brown with white stripes, like he'd described.

"When I said I wanted a real car, he reminded me that he'd asked if I wanted a good *model* car. Only on the phone, I thought he said, a *good* model car. But that's a used car salesman for you!

"Jimmie and I have been good friends ever since."

When the mayor called on Jimmie for a response, he said only six words: "See you in the funny papers!"

And you will, at every twist and turn in Tinyburg, likely run into this likable Peter Pan, who refuses to grow up because he observes how the years tend to turn some people bitter and sour.

One final word about Jimmie Swan, the dishwasher at the Tinyburg Nursing Home. Dr. Gordon, the town's physician, says he sees less of Jimmie than any patient he's ever treated.

It seems that Jimmie's found a secret prescription of his own, tucked away in the Bible in Proverbs 17:22. It reads, "A merry heart doeth good like a medicine."

An Early Halloween

The Preacher at the Tinyburg Church finally decided to enroll in one the the Church Growth conferences led by the Reverend Henry Moss, doctor of divinity.

Dr. Moss, pastor of the Bigtown Church, charges $50 for his one-day workshops, claiming they're easily worth $250. Suspicious that Dr. Moss is more of a showman than a minister, the Preacher had until now avoided the workshops.

He also felt a little uneasy about Dr. Moss' February Bible seminars in Hawaii, as well as his frequent tours to the Holy Land. The Hawaii brochures said more about moonlight cruises, beach cook-outs, swimming, sunning, and island-hopping than the Bible. He wondered how Dr. Moss could keep his fingers in so many pies.

Nevertheless, Dr. Moss preached to large crowds, and now that his morning services were televised, he was more popular. So one September morning, the Preacher appeared at the Bigtown Church with his $50 for a growth seminar.

Dr. Moss began by saying that in this television and mass media era, churches must capture the eye of the public. He warned that too many services are boring:

"In most churches, folks have memorized exactly what's to be said and at what minute it's said. I wager some of your members know your prayers backward as well as forward. Brethren, get out of the rut. Here at Bigtown last July 4, we put on a spectacular. Church couldn't hold the people. We put a hundred children and youth in a mass choir, wearing blue, white, and red blouses and shirts. Arranged them like the American flag. You talk about something to knock your eyes out!

"Brethren, when you get a hundred youngsters all decked out in red, white, and blue, you've got two hundred parents there to see them, and a hundred or so grandparents, plus another hundred brothers and sisters, and before you know it, men, you've got you a crowd."

Dr. Moss then projected on a screen the nine letters of the word *different*. Then he continued, "To illustrate, think of eleven key words, beginning with one of these letters. Here are the first eleven words that come to my mind:

> D-aring
> I -nnovative
> F-un
> F-antastic
> E-xciting
> R-efreshing
> E-ntertaining
> N-ovel
> T-rendy

Elaborating on each word, he said churches must dream big: "Don't just copy my methods. Create new ministries of your own. Convert your congregation into a trend-setting church, rather than bringing up the rear. Take the Preacher from Tinyburg, whom I see in the audience. Even in that jumping-off place where he serves, he can think of something new that would, for example, set the trend for Ebenezer Church, a sister church out in the country. Or, maybe set the pace for the struggling little congregation at nearby Pretense."

During the noon hour, the Preacher from Tinyburg took a walk downtown, where a sign fascinated him, "Costumes Unlimited, Inc." Curious, he stepped inside and discovered it was a rental agency for theatrical costumes. "We rent to high school drama groups and the like," a clerk explained. "Also to communities that stage centennials or reunions—anything where folks dress up. And we rent all varieties for Halloween parties and such events where party-goers like to masquerade."

One costume quickly caught the Preacher's eye—a red devil's suit, complete with a long tail and a mask with pointed ears. It was designed to fit tightly, something like a monkey suit. Slowly the wheels of the Preacher's fertile imagination began to spin. Hadn't Dr. Moss promised that if he sprung new ideas on the Tinyburg Church, he'd see dramatic growth and also set the trend for Ebenezer and Pretense churches?

So before you could say "The devil made me do it," he rented the fancy, red outfit for the weekend.

On his way home, he stopped to see S. Franklin Rodd, a farmer, and borrow his pitchfork. His next stop was at Carl Bradley's, who does wood-carving as a hobby, and asked if he could design him a sandwich sign, "the kind you suspend over your shoulders with ropes, with lettering on the sign-boards that hang down in front and back."

Carl said yes, also agreeing to paint the front of the sign, "Don't attend this church." The back side would read, "Satanic Forces at Work Here." Carl was puzzled over their purpose, but the Preacher mumbled something about Halloween and pledged Carl to secrecy.

The next day was Friday, a bright day in September, a touch of fall in the air, a sort of early Halloween feeling in one's bones. When the Preacher left the house that morning, he told his wife Carol he wouldn't be home for dinner: "Got some errands to do—then a few holes of golf. May not be home until dark—so don't wait supper."

Shortly after noon, making sure no one was in the church building, he changed into the devil's suit. It was a tight fit, but by removing all of his clothing except his underwear briefs, he squeezed in. Next he fitted the sandwich sign over his shoulders, picked up the pitchfork which he'd stored in a closet, and walked outside. He was glad no one saw him come out of the church, lest they guess who he was. Then he paced slowly up and down the sidewalk, in front and alongside the church.

If this doesn't create enough curiosity to fill the pews on Sunday, then I'm an angel with wings, he said to himself. He fantasized how next September, Dr. Moss might invite him to speak at his Growth Workshop.

As hoped, the Preacher in the devil suit drew attention. Passers-by stopped to gawk, wondering if their eyes were going bad. There were two or three near-collisions, as drivers braked suddenly at the sight. Word spread around town and, about 2:30, the mobile unit of radio TINY-FM came by for a live, remote description. At 3:00 PM, the television station in Bigtown called the church office about sending a camera crew over, so the parading devil could be seen on the evening news.

At 3:10 PM, Aunt Sarah Biggs turned the corner on her way home from a class potluck. Throwing up her arms in surprise and dropping her casserole dish on the sidewalk, where it broke with a loud crash, she exclaimed, "All my life I heard warnings from the pulpit that the devil's after us; but who knew I'd live to see him in the flesh?"

School buses were re-routed by the church, so the children could see the strange sight. And at 4:00 PM, Uncle Billy Cutrell, who'd been taking a nap on the back porch of his home across the street, was awakened by the snickering of three boys about ten and eleven. One of them was Mark, the Preacher's youngest son. Raising up on his elbow to watch, Uncle Billy was surprised they were in his tomato patch: "What you boys doing?"

"Nothing," replied Mark, innocently. "We're not bothering your good tomatoes—just the rotten ones. The devil's after Daddy's church, and we're going to rotten-egg him!"

"The imagination of modern youth is a mystery to me," Uncle Billy mumbled to himself. "Another proof of the evil of television."

Curious, Uncle Billy walked around the house just in time to see three rotten tomatoes smack the front of the sandwich sign, while red juice ran down the letters, "Don't attend this church." It reminded him of blood. He thought of sermons he'd heard on the blood of Christ, how the church was bought by the blood of the Lamb. And now he was seeing it in living color!

But the devil, or whoever it was, said nothing. He made no attempt to avoid a second barrage of tomato missiles, but merely turned slowly and walked in the opposite direction. This revealed the other side of the sign, "Satanic Forces at Work Here."

"Satanic forces my eye," Uncle Billy muttered. "This is some idiot who thinks he can tear down in one afternoon what we've struggled to build for a generation."

"Mister Whoever-You-Are," he ordered in a pompous tone.

"I'm giving you sixty seconds to get off private, church property. And that's an order, not a request." The imitation devil, appearing not to hear, continued to pace back and forth.

Getting no response, and a little apprehensive of the sharp pitchfork on the devil's shoulder, Uncle Billy wheeled around and walked the three short blocks to the Tinyburg Police. "We know all about it," the chief reassured Uncle Billy. "Down there earlier this afternoon. Nothing we can do. That sidewalk's public property. Can't arrest someone for wearing a costume. Probably a member of the Lions Club, publicizing a Halloween stunt of some kind."

"It's not Halloween and it's not private property and it's not funny," Uncle Billy shot back. "I want that man, or whatever it is, arrested."

"Arrested for what?"

"For several things—obstructing traffic, public nuisance, interfering with freedom of worship, trespassing. Enough violations to send him to the state penitentiary—maybe a federal prison."

"Uncle Billy, if you want to assume the risk of false accusation, you'll have to swear out a warrant for his arrest. You willing?"

"You bet a Halloween Jack-o-Lantern I'm willing," replied Uncle Billy, pulling out a ballpoint pen as if he were ready to sign the Declaration of Independence.

When Tinyburg's only police car pulled up in front of the church, the first thing the officer did was to order the devil to remove his mask, which he did. Laughing, the officer asked Uncle Billy if he still wanted him arrested, since the "devil" was his own minister.

"Certainly. If nothing else, any man of God who'd dress up in an outfit like this needs a sanity test anyway. He needs protection against himself. Who knows what he'll try next?"

By the time the officer, Uncle Billy, and the Preacher reached the city jail, Uncle Billy changed his mind. "I'll withdraw the charges," he agreed, "if this yahoo we call a Preacher promises me to act like a grown man. No doubt the congregation will be calling for his resignation, so no point in adding a jail sentence to his misery.

"Oh, one other thing. I insist he remove that outfit here and now. I don't want him parading home with his tail dragging the sidewalk like a monkey.

"But Uncle Billy, I don't have any . . . or that is, not many clothes on underneath," the Preacher begged. "Since my costume fit so tight, I left them at the church."

"Then it's jail or public nakedness, take your choice," Uncle Billy exploded. "Makes little difference to me."

Which explains why, once he took off the devil's suit, the Preacher hid in a back room of the police station until good dark. Then the police car drove him as close as possible to a side entrance of the church, where he made a dash for the door and his clothes. To this day, he's known as Tinyburg's first streaking Preacher.

In spite of the uproar he'd caused, the Preacher was rewarded on Sunday morning when he saw every pew filled, plus some worshipers standing. Uncle Billy, looking for his accustomed pew, found it taken. "I'm not surprised," he said to himself. "When you change the House of the Lord into a circus of freaks, you can expect the riff-raff to turn out and fill every seat."

The congregation was anxious for the sermon, curious as to what their minister would say. A few speculated he might attempt to wear the devil's suit in the pulpit. His remarks were simple, but disarming. He quoted the Bible as teaching that Satan sometimes goes around as a roaring lion, seeking whom he might devour. At other times he appears as an angel, or messenger of light, deceiving everyone.

Then he continued: "Beloved, if Satan ever comes to Tinyburg in the flesh, let me assure you he won't wear traditional garb. He'll wear a disguise to make himself look innocent. And he won't carry a pitchfork. More likely it'll be a Bible, the biggest he can find, with gold edges. Now let me ask which is worse: a Preacher dressing up for fun, like the devil? Or the devil dressing up for real, like a preacher?"

There was a long pause, then silence. Uncle Billy cocked his head, squinted his eyes at the sunlight filtering through a stained glass window, and said to himself, "Guess we've got about the smartest Preacher here in Tinyburg that ever opened the Good Book. He can find the cleverest ways to make his point."

And with that remark, he erased the incident from his mind and never mentioned it again. Except that each fall, as Halloween nears, he keeps a sharp eye for anything unusual around the church. "Never know," he told Aunt Sarah when he ran into her buying a new casserole dish at the Tinyburg Variety Store. "We could see angels and Seraphim, right here on the streets of Tinyburg."

The Reverend Doctor Henry Moss has never invited the Preacher to speak at one of his Growth Seminars. The gossip is he can't tolerate anyone who upstages him, especially from an out-of-the-way place such as Tinyburg, population 1,473.

An Empty Easter

Don't allow the title of this story to fool you. Easter is a time of fullness and victory. But a part of that fullness is emptiness. To explain, let's go back to an Easter in Tinyburg, years ago.

Greg Thompson, the first native of Tinyburg to earn a Ph.D. degree, was an eight-year-old at the time, and a member of his Aunt Opal Baggett's Sunday School class.

"Now children," Opal announced in late February, "Easter's coming, when we celebrate the resurrection of Jesus. Easter arrives in the spring, when all of nature explodes in new life.

"To help us understand how Easter means life, I'm giving you a project for Palm Sunday. You have six weeks to think about it. On that Sunday before Easter, I'm asking each of you to bring—in a box or sack—something that's alive, such as a pet or plant. I hope each brings something different."

Opal's assignment excited the youngsters, and on Palm Sunday, each brought a container of some kind, such as a shoe box, cereal box, or grocery carton. As you'd expect, one child brought a baby chicken, while another brought a tiny bunny rabbit. There was also a young oak seedling, a parakeet, a goldfish in a pail of water, a baby kitten, plus assorted bugs and worms.

The class played "Show-n-Tell," as each boy and girl carefully opened the top to his carton to share what was inside. And each time, Opal reminded them that life, and living things, is what Easter's all about.

Finally it was Greg's turn. Since no sounds had come from his box, such as chirping, squealing, or scratching, everyone was curious. Carefully he opened the lid, acting as if something ferocious might spring out. But no! The box was empty.

"What happened to your little pet?" asked his Aunt Opal, thinking that whatever he'd brought from home had fallen out or escaped.

"Oh, it's supposed to be empty!" Greg explained. "Remember how Jesus' tomb was empty on the first Easter morning? If His body had been inside the tomb, it would have been a dead one."

None of the other children caught the significance of what Greg said. Even Opal wondered how an eight-year-old boy could come up with such a mature insight. So as best she could, she helped the other children understand.

After church services that morning, she asked the Preacher if he'd like to see Greg's box. He, too, marveled at the insight of Greg, saying to his aunt, "I'd never thought that one of the best examples of life, especially at Easter, is something that's empty."

All week, the Preacher thought about Greg's empty shoe box. Since the week before Easter is always a busy time with a big community-wide service on Good Friday, the Preacher had finalized his Easter sermon ten days earlier. It was a scholarly message, tracing the burial customs of Bible times, how Jesus' body was prepared for burial, the kinds of spices used, embalming methods of the ancient Egyptians, and the like.

But when Easter morning came and the Preacher stood in the pulpit of the Tinyburg Church, every pew filled and running over, he laid aside his carefully prepared notes.

"Friends," he began, "excuse me for not giving a traditional Easter sermon. Instead, I want to talk to you out of my heart. Walk with me as I retrace my steps of this past week.

"Last Sunday, one of Opal Baggett's Sunday School boys showed me an empty shoe box. It was an Easter project, a class assignment. I didn't see the point until he explained, 'The empty box represents Jesus' empty tomb.' And in that moment, I saw anew that fullness in the Christian life starts with emptiness.

"Let me explain further as I tell you some of the things I did this week.

"On Monday, I came here in the sanctuary to look for a notebook I'd misplaced. It was so quiet and peaceful, the morning sun streaming through the stained glass windows. I sat in one of the pews and just listened. With my heart, I mean—not my ears. Have you ever sat a few minutes in an empty church? You should. I felt God so close. I felt His presence fill the entire sanctuary. I don't mean I want to worship regularly in an empty church building. But there's something about a quiet church, with no one listening or watching, that get's next to you. I felt a fullness of God's presence in an empty room, and the memory of that fullness stayed with me all day.

"Late Tuesday afternoon, I was raking the lawn, so the new grass can grow better. I picked up an old bird's nest that fell from a tree during one of last winter's storms. A few little feathers were mingled with the tiny bits of grass and twigs that lined the nest. At first I was sad, as I thought about last summer's baby birds. Then I remembered that an empty nest means those tiny birds grew strong enough to fly on their own, and that in cold January, they were down south, chirping and singing, and this very day are making their way back to Tinyburg. The fullness of a robin's breast comes only after the nest is empty. What a strange world if birds never grew up to leave their nests.

"On Wednesday, I drove to the state penitentiary for a Holy Week service. The chaplain, who's a good friend, invites me over for special occasions. As we walked past a row of cells, I noticed one that was empty. I remembered the inmate—a seventeen-year-old boy who foolishly stole a car and wrecked it.

"What happened to him? The chaplain told how he had been freed on early-release probation, after assuring officials he had a job and would make full restitution. I can't tell you how proud I was to see that empty cell. We need prisons, but after a lawbreaker pays his debt to society, how good it looks to see an empty cell. I rejoiced because that inmate was free— free to begin a new life, to prove himself. Out of emptiness came the promise of fullness.

"On Thursday, I attended a wedding. It was an emotional wedding, in a good sense. The bride was one of five children— the first in her family to marry. I watched while the mother hugged and told her goodbye, as she and her new husband left on their honeymoon. The eyes of both parents were swimming in tears.

"At first, as I looked at the mother's empty arms, I felt sorry for her. Then I told myself that children, like birds, are born to grow up and leave home and form their own families. Moms and Dads can't hold on to them forever. Good parenting is preparing for that day when we turn our kids loose. Out of the emptiness of her parents' arms, this beautiful bride was finding fullness and completeness in the arms of her new husband.

"On Friday, I visited one of our members in the hospital. Three days earlier, he'd been on the critical list. So imagine my feelings when I stepped in his hospital room and the patient was gone. My first fear was that he had died. But praise God, I was mistaken. He'd been discharged! He had improved dramatically, even to the surprise of his doctor. His bed was empty, and I was glad.

"The best use of hospital beds is to help us get well, not die on. The empty bed in that room spoke to me—it said my friend was better, free to go home. Out of the emptiness of a hospital bed was the promise of fullness of health.

"Friends, it seems that wherever I turned this week, I saw something empty—an empty bird nest, vacant prison cell, empty hospital bed, an empty church, and yes, empty arms of proud parents. And each has preached its own message, just like Greg's empty shoe box. Today, I appreciate more than ever the meaning of the first Easter, symbolized by an empty tomb."

At the dinner table the Preacher's oldest son, Mark, questioned his logic. "Dad," he began, "your ideas about emptiness don't make sense. Suppose I go to the refrigerator for a glass of milk and the carton's empty. Or I write a check and the bank account's empty. Or I get in the car to go on a date and it won't start, because the gas tank is empty?"

"Mark," he replied, "I'm not saying everything's good just because it's empty. That would place a premium on, say, ignorance or empty-headedness. It's what a thing is empty of that makes the difference. A cell empty of a prisoner spells freedom. A hospital bed empty of a patient spells health. An empty tomb in Jerusalem spells eternal life."

"I see your point," nodded Mark. "Maybe you need eight-year-old Greg for an assistant pastor to help you with more sermon ideas."

"Heaven knows I need all the good ideas I can get," the Preacher smiled, as he emptied the platter of Easter ham into Mark's plate.

A Phone Call from God

The Preacher announced that on the first Sunday in April, he'd play a recording of a telephone call from God: "I can't reveal the name of our member who got the call, but I assure you the recording's genuine. No tricks, no April fooling."

Curiosity mounted as the date drew near. A few skeptics said it was a cheap promotional gimmick. Others saw it as a creative effort by the Preacher to say old truths in a new way.

On the appointed Sunday, following the song service, the Preacher walked to the pulpit and pushed the "on" button to his tape recorder, wired to play through the sound system.

"First," he explained, "I want to emphasize this is an actual conversation, taped here in Tinyburg. All I've edited out is the name of the family. On the tape, they're just John and Mary Doe. Is everyone listening? This may be your *only* chance to listen in on a phone call from God."

With that, he switched on the audiocassette and took his seat. You can imagine how quiet everyone was as they listened:

"Hello! Hello! Yes, this is John Doe in Tinyburg. What's that? You're calling long distance from Heaven? Who do I know in heaven and how did you get my number? Said your name's God? Course I know you. Known you all my life. Been a member of Tinyburg Church since I was a teenager.

"You say how I'm getting along? Tolerable, considering everything. How about yourself? Had any spring weather up there? Oh, excuse me. I should have known it's always spring in heaven. I wasn't thinking.

"What's that? You haven't heard from me lately? You know, Lord, I told my wife the other night, I said, Hon, we should get down here on our knees right now and say our bedtime

126

prayers. But then I got to watchin' ole Johnny Carson. You ever watch him? Boy, is he funny. Before I knew it, it was way past our bedtime. I wish to goodness we'd gone ahead and prayed anyway. Yes, I promise to start saying my prayers this very night, whether I need to or not.

"How's that? You mean how much I give to the Tinyburg Church? No problem. Just finished my income tax and claimed donations last year of $62. No, that's not for a month, for a year. Twelve months.

"You say that averages just a little over a dollar a week? You need to call our members who give loose change—dimes and quarters. Me, I always give folding money. At least a dollar. Sometimes two or three. What did I pay for our new TV? Not nearly what some of my neighbors shell out for those fancy cabinet models with stereo, radio, VCR and everything. I don't believe we paid much over $300 for our little ole set.

"What you must understand, Lord, is that we're in a recession down here. For me and the wife, it's turned into a *de*pression. Then you take our unexpected expenses. Something always needs fixing. We'll never see daylight again.

"Was I in church the second Sunday in February? How could I, with all the streets iced up? Being in the weather department, you remember that ice storm that hit Tinyburg on Saturday night. Never thawed a drop 'till Wednesday. Did I get out for work on Monday? You bet I did. Couldn't afford to miss. I work for *my* living.

"Oh, I knew you'd get around to the Preacher's sermons. Sure I listen. What did he preach on last Sunday? You caught me off guard, there. Let's see, what was it? Lord, that's been nearly a week ago, and so much has happened. You know, important things that occupy a fellow's time. I think he talked mostly about the Bible—you know, Luke or John. No, maybe it was Corinthians. Somewhere over there in the New Testament, but those funny Bible names slip my tongue.

"Sir? I have trouble understanding you. Must be a bad connection. Did I hear you'd been in jail? You wouldn't kid me, Lord? Course you haven't been in jail. If so, the news would be all over the papers and radio. You told about it in the Bible? Where? Matthew? What chapter? Yes, I'll look it up. Hold the phone . . . (long pause) . . . sorry to keep you waiting, but would you believe my Bible got put back in the closet, had to dig it out.

"Let's see here, you said Matthew 25:43? Where is Matthew? Old Testament or New? How do you spell Matthew? Never can remember. Comes right after Malachi? Maybe they left him out of this Bible.

"Oh, here it is, 'I was . . . sick, and in prison, and ye visited me not.' Lord, you're kidding, even if it is in the Bible. No one ever heard of God going to jail. You say to skip on down to verse 45? Yes, here it is, 'Inasmuch as ye did it not to one of the least of these, ye did it not to me.'

"You mean to tell me that whenever any low-down, no-count skalawag gets locked up, that's the same as You being in jail? And the way to visit You in prison is to visit someone else who's there?

"You must be joking. Those bums in jail can rot, as far as I care. I say lock 'em up and throw the key away. Good riddance. Ninety percent of those turned loose are back in jail in a week. You say I'm exaggerating? Maybe. But I don't see a good Christian man like myself hanging around jail houses. That's why they have their own chaplains . . . . but if you insist, sure, I'll ask the sheriff about visiting hours.

"You say you've got another question or two? If you don't mind, let me sit down. I'm not used to talking on the phone so long.

"Do I gossip about my neighbors? No siree. Anything I say about them they deserve, maybe more. These Tinyburg folks aren't saints, you know. Don't you believe in telling the truth, let the chips fall where they will? But one thing I'm sure of. When I share something that I know's the gospel truth, I ask that person to swear they won't tell another soul. I don't want them running all over town, talking mean about our neighbors, even if they are no count.

"You say you got one last question? Okay, shoot! Do I have a job in my church? I'm sure glad you asked that, Lord, for I'm right in the middle of everything. Why, if anyone tells me things is going on in our church that shouldn't be, I'm the first one to go down and jump all over the Preacher. And I tell him exactly what I think.

"You say that isn't what you have in mind? You mean something like teaching a Bible class or visiting old people? I'd love to Lord, the best in the world. But you see, I ain't got no talent. I get all nervous around church people. Yes, I'm an officer in the Tinyburg Lions Club. But that's different. My business contacts are in that club. Part of my meat and bread. My club duties is almost like going to work in the morning.

"Besides, no one asks me to do anything at church. Lots of snobbish members on the roll. Little cliques, you know. The nominating committee last fall? Oh, I forgot them. Something must be wrong with my thinking cap.

"Now that you mention it, the committee *did* ask me to take an office. Slips my mind, what it was. But no matter, they found someone else. At my age, it's time to slow down, let the young people shoulder the load us older members been carrying for years. You know what I mean—you've been around a while, yourself.

"Well thanks for calling. Sure good to hear your voice. And if you're ever in Tinyburg, stop by and say hello."

And so ended the recording heard in morning worship at the Tinyburg Church. However, the Preacher said he wanted to play one more short tape. It was recorded after John Doe said goodbye to God. Here's how it went:

"Hello, operator? Give me the long distance operator. That you? This is John Doe in Tinyburg. Just got a call from Heaven. Yes, I said heaven, spelled h-e-a-v-e-n. What's the area code? How do I know? But it *is* long distance. How far? Beat's me. But it's far enough. I guess we talked half an hour. What I need to know is, look at my record and see if God called me collect. He didn't? Boy, what a relief! Thanks for checking. Goodbye."

(At this point, there was a short gap, then a conversation between John Doe and his wife.)

". . . say, Hon, what was it you were asking? Who was on the phone? Never mind, you wouldn't believe me if I told you. But I tell you one thing—next time the phone rings, you answer, for you needed that call lots worse than me.

"Was it a wrong number? Not by a long shot. Believe me, that fellow's got my number. In fact, He has the numbers of most folks in Tinyburg."

A Bus Trip to Bluesville

A dream come true! The senior adults of the Tinyburg Church were off on a bus trip to Bluesville, country music capital of the world.

"Never thought I'd live to see where all that music comes from," boasted George Mason, one of the first to buy a ticket. George owns a barbershop which he calls "The Purple Crackerbox." If you don't like country music, go somewhere else for a haircut, because his radio keeps tuned to Bluesville.

George also collects photographs of country and western stars. He clips these from record albums, flyers, and magazines. Each photo is mounted on a cardboard cut out in the shape of a star. These practically cover the walls of his barbershop. He dreams of the day when he can display a full-color, glossy photo of Polly Darton, autographed.

Of the thirty-five oldsters on the trip, only one was under the age of fifty-five: Jimmie Swan, twenty-eight, dishwasher at the Tinyburg Nursing Home.

Clay Barker discouraged Jimmie, suggesting he take a vacation with friends his age.

But Jimmie argued, "I like older people—work with them every day. And Myrtle Eagleton will need help getting her wheelchair on and off the bus."

So on the appointed day, the bus pulled away from the church parking lot with thirty-four senior citizens and one young adult, bound for Bluesville.

Their reservations were at a luxury hotel on Melody Lane. Checking in was easy because with group reservations, their rooms were preassigned. In minutes, fast elevators whisked them to the fourteenth floor, which gave them a stunning view of the city, the glittering lights of the theaters, and the souvenir shops. Their rooms were in a block, numbered 1421 to 1457.

Jimmie Swan, who roomed with Uncle Billy, was the last to arrive, since he took the stairs.

"You mean you're walking up fourteen flights?" asked the bell captain.

Jimmie, too timid to admit that his claustrophobia makes him scared of elevators, pretended he needed the exercise.

As Jimmie bounded up the steps, he counted the floors, watching for the fourteenth. After climbing twelve flights, he saw the sign, *14th floor*. "This can't be," he said, although Uncle Billy was waiting in a room marked 1450 on what everyone assumed was the fourteenth floor. "You miscounted," Uncle Billy said as he adjusted the frigid air conditioning, which made him feel it was January instead of July.

"I *can* count to thirteen," Jimmie said sharply. "I may not be as smart as you, but I know the difference in thirteen and fourteen."

"Hold on," Uncle Billy cautioned. "No harm meant. 'Course you can count to thirteen. So what? It's a nice room, whatever the number."

"I'm going to find out for sure," Jimmie said as he dialed the front desk.

"Yes, Mr. Swan, you're in the right room on the right floor," explained the clerk. "The truth is, since some guests are superstitious, we have no thirteenth floor. In our numbering, we skip from the twelfth to the fourteenth floor. Does this upset you?"

"Not me," replied Jimmie. "I wanted to prove to my roommate I can count to thirteen!"

Just then, Aunt Sarah Biggs knocked on their door. "Where's the ice dispenser? I'm dying for a cold drink."

"Give me your ice bucket," Jimmie volunteered. "I'll find some. By the way, Aunt Sarah, do you know we're all on the thirteenth floor?"

"Silly boy, it says plainly on the door that this is room 1450."

But when Jimmie quoted the desk clerk, Aunt Sarah lost all interest in ice buckets and cold drinks. Taking the elevator to the lobby, she confronted the clerk:

"Sir, you misled us good people from Tinyburg. You put us on the wrong floor. We demand new rooms, right now."

"I don't understand."

"Well I understand," she replied. "You put us on floor thirteen and called it fourteen. And anybody knows that thirteen is unlucky. All kinds of mischief can happen. Myrtle could slip in a bathtub, the hotel catch on fire, a bed break down, poison gas come in through the vents, or . . ."

Other guests in line, alarmed at talk of poison gas and fire, turned to listen. The assistant manager, who overheard the conversation, rushed quickly to Aunt Sarah's side and invited her to step into his office.

It was a plush office, with thick carpeting and oversize, autographed photos of music stars, including one of Polly Darton in full color.

"We're pleased to have you as a guest, Miss Biggs," he began. "How can we make you comfortable?"

"Right now I'm interested in safety, not comfort. We want rooms on another floor, all thirty-five of us from Tinyburg."

"Miss Biggs," he said, in a low, confidential tone, "ours is the most popular hotel on Melody Lane, booked solid for six months. Every room's full. There's no way we can shift thirty-five guests. What we can do is refund your deposit, but if you leave, you'll have to break up your group to find a room here and a room there."

"I'm not moving, nor am I sleeping on the thirteenth floor," she replied, raising her voice with each sentence. "If necessary, I'll sleep in the bus on the parking lot. But if I do, I'll put a big sign on the windshield, 'Yes, Virginia, there *is* a 13th floor!'"

"Shh, shh. Please, Miss Biggs. Don't raise your voice. Remember the other guests. Now be reasonable. I *can't* give you another room. But if you'll keep quiet about the number thirteen, the hotel will give you a free room for three nights. Plus all your meals and a $50 voucher to spend in our gift shop. Is that fair?"

Aunt Sarah thought a minute, looking at the framed photos on the wall. "Maybe I can sit up for three nights without sleep for that much money, providing you throw in a bonus."

"Like what?"

"Like that autographed photo of Polly Darton!"

"It's a deal," smiled the assistant manager.

The three days in Bluesville passed like three hours. Never had the Tinyburg folks enjoyed so much fun, although Aunt Sarah's friends wondered about the circles under her eyes. She gave a simple answer: "You know how it is when you're away from home—you never sleep as well in a strange bed."

In addition to the shows, the group enjoyed browsing in the souvenir stores. They saw thousands of memorabilia of the stars—rhinestone belt buckles, salt shakers, ash trays, T-shirts, paper weights, pictures, posters, calendars, cigarette lighters, cups, dishes, tumblers, glasses, saucers, knives, records, cassette tapes, videos, calculators, combs, brushes, pillows, ball point pens, rulers and yardsticks, golf balls, picture post cards, books, magazines, wallets, purses, beach balls, balloons, and mirrors!

Also belts, mugs, picture frames, nail clippers, cigarette lighters, bumper stickers, tooth pick holders, wallets, coin holders, wall plaques, caps, salt-and-pepper shakers, mottoes, key chains, costume jewelry, pocket knives, and bottle openers.

Everywhere, tourists gawked, babies cried, and kids squealed, caught up in the make-believe magic of country music.

Also fascinating were the exhibits of paraphernalia once owned by the stars: boots, dressing gowns, guitars, western hats, fringed vests, string ties, and even antique cars.

"When the Stars Come Out" was the favorite show on Melody Lane. George Mason, the barber, liked the show so well he saw it three times.

Imagine his pleasure when Aunt Sarah presented him with the photo of Polly Darton she won as a bonus to stay on the thirteenth floor. "But where did you get it?" he stammered. "Trade secret," she winked.

On the trip home, Aunt Sarah whispered to the driver, "Stop at a good steak house with a salad bar and I'll pay the tab." Grateful for surviving three nights on the thirteenth floor, she wanted to treat her friends with her refund money.

"But Aunt Sarah, you can't afford thirty-five meals," Uncle Billy sympathized, as they got off the bus.

"Don't tell me what I can afford or not afford," she smiled.

Standing in line, Clay Barker whispered to Uncle Billy, "I'll bet you $50 you can't eat some of all fifty items on that buffet."

"You serious, Clay Barker?"

"As serious as a boy who's just flunked the fifth grade," Clay replied.

"Then you might as well get out your wallet, because I'm about to prove I can eat a serving of everything. Imagine, being paid to eat all you want!"

Clay called a bus boy aside and asked for one of the oversize platters used for Texas size steaks. Pointing to Uncle Billy he explained, "He's got a tape worm; takes lots to fill him up."

On his first trip to the salad bar, Uncle Billy served himself four bowls of soup—vegetarian beef, split pea, cream of mushroom, and French onion, plus assorted crackers of every imaginable shape. "That soup's a meal in itself," he confided to Clay, wiping his mouth. But Clay reminded him he'd just started!

On the second trip he selected fresh spinach and shredded lettuce, topping it with asparagus, broccoli, pickled beets, cauliflower, shredded carrots, celery sticks, cucumber slices, sweet and dill pickles, fresh green onions, thick slices of white and yellow onions, black and green olives, slices of green peppers, tiny pickled peppers, radishes, sliced tomatoes and tiny cocktail tomatoes, shirred boiled eggs, grated cheese, alfalfa sprouts, bean sprouts, bacon bits, sunflower seeds, dried soybeans, raisins, and peanuts, topped with eight salad dressings.

Since each dressing also came in low-calorie, this made sixteen servings in all: vinegar and oil, mayonnaise, Roquefort, Thousand Island, French, Italian, Russian, and Blue Cheese.

By now others were finished and the bus driver was blowing his horn. "Patience! Patience!" Clay Barker hollered out the restaurant door. "Give an old man time to eat his dinner."

Returning for his third trip, Uncle Billy sampled each of the prepared salads: cole slaw, apple sauce, cottage cheese, potato salad, macaroni salad, pea salad, six bean salad, Waldorf salad, taco salad, three flavors of plain jello (strawberry, orange, and grape), plus the same three flavors with fruit cocktail.

Although the driver continued to blow his horn, causing other customers to wonder what was wrong, Uncle Billy rushed to the fruit bar for his fourth and last trip. He helped himself to wedges of watermelon, fresh pineapple, cantaloupe, and honey dew melon, plus a bunch of grapes, whole strawberries dusted with powdered sugar, bananas sliced in strawberry juice, orange and apple slices, prunes, and assorted canned fruits (peaches, cherries, pears, fruit cocktail, blackberries, grapefruit sections, and gooseberries).

At this point the bus driver stormed inside and told Clay and Uncle Billy he was leaving, but they could catch a Greyhound bus due in an hour. "Hold your horses!" cried Uncle Billy, filling a doggie bag with fresh fruits to eat on the bus: a banana, apple, orange, pear, and plum.

It was only three more hours to Tinyburg, but it was long enough for Uncle Billy to promise God that if He'd cure his stomachache, he'd never eat at another salad bar. And at a rest stop, he inquired of the driver where he could buy some Pepto-Bismol!

At dusk, the chartered bus rolled into Tinyburg, along with three closely guarded secrets. Clay Barker never told his wife he lost $50 on a bet to Uncle Billy. Aunt Sarah never told how she got the autographed photo. Nor that she paid for the thirty-five "free" meals by sitting up three nights in her hotel room.

But what everyone did know and appreciate was the suspended beauty of the evening star in the western sky, which had just come into view. Soon it was followed by dozens of other stars, then hundreds, and finally thousands. Spontaneously, the group broke into singing:

> Tell me why the stars do shine?
> Tell me why the ivy twine?
> Tell me why the sky's so blue?
> And I will tell you just why I love you.

Jimmie Swan helped the senior citizens unload their luggage as they greeted friends and relatives, there to pick them up. At first, no one wanted to say good-bye, to break the spell, as if they knew something precious was now history. George Mason, clutching the autographed photo of Polly Darton under his arm, expressed their feelings: "The stars over Tinyburg are brighter than all the stars and glitter of Bluesville."

One by one the cars and pickup trucks carried them home, down the tree-shaded streets and country roads. Aunt Sarah, heavy with sleep, was the first traveler in bed, never bothering to turn on a light or brush her teeth.

George Mason, too excited to sleep, was the last in bed. He took time for a short walk around the block, humming to himself:

> Will there be any stars,
> any stars in my crown?

When at evening the sun goeth down?
When I wake with the blest
In the mansions of rest,
Will there be any stars in my crown?

E. E. HEWITT

    Once George finally turned off the lights and went to bed, all was silent in the village and the stars had the night to themselves.

Rev. Dawg Gets a Doctorate

The Reverend Doctor Henry Moss, minister of the Bigtown Church in Bigtown, is an egotist. Everyone knows that. But since he's egotistical in a naive sort of way, most folks, including the Preacher at the nearby Tinyburg Church, tend to smile at his faults.

Reverend Moss has his fingers in many pies. Energetic and restless, he needs more outlets for his creativity than his pastorate offers him. Among other projects, he organizes and escorts one tour group after another to the Holy Land, plus midwinter Bible seminars in Hawaii.

At one time, Reverend Moss was a field representative (call that "broker") for the Metaphysical School of Heavenly Learning in California. For $100, Reverend Moss promised a doctor's degree by return mail for anyone able to sign his name, other than with an X.

So the Preacher showed no surprise when a fat, colorful envelope arrived at the Tinyburg post office from Reverend Moss, offering a new series of doctor's degrees for half-price, only $50. It read:

"I've just been elected president of the International Seminary of Pretense. We base our degrees on experience. If a minister has already benefited from the school of experience, sitting in a classroom is a waste of time."

The Preacher smiled at the sales pitch. "Same old Reverend Moss," he sighed. "Anyone knows that Pretense, just seven miles from here, no longer has a high school, to say nothing of a seminary."

"Oh, I know that," Reverend Moss replied when the Preacher called for details. "We don't operate a full-blown campus at Pretense—just a post office box for our mail. But the degrees are genuine. No, we don't have a faculty. Our graduates come from the school of life, the best there is."

When Reverend Moss asked if he wished to nominate a candidate, the Preacher said he was in a hurry to go rabbit hunting and didn't have time to talk. It was a crisp, fall day, and he couldn't wait to change into some old clothes and take Dennis rabbit-hunting.

Dennis, a beagle hound, lives for two pleasures: to sleep in the sun on the Preacher's back porch and to chase rabbits. I say chase, for Dennis has yet to catch one!

The Preacher was putting out a fresh bowl of water for Dennis when, on an impulse, he asked, "Dennis, how would you like to have a doctor's degree of your very own?"

Dennis, unimpressed, licked his lips and wagged his tail.

Oh, I forgot to say that "Reverend Dennis" is the dog's nickname. A band of white around his neck that looks like a clerical collar gave the Preacher the idea for the name.

A few days later on a business trip to Bigtown, the Preacher, just for fun, stopped by to see the Reverend Moss.

"Just found a candidate in Tinyburg for a doctorate," he began, with mock excitement in his voice. "How do you apply?"

"My good friend, you're right where you're supposed to be if you want a degree from the International Seminary of Pretense." Before the words were out of his mouth, Reverend Moss reached for an application and spread it on his desk. "What's the candidate's name?"

"Dennis. Dennis Dawg. Reverend Dennis Dawg, that is."

Reverend Moss looked up in surprise: "You mean Dog like in d-o-g?"

"No, he spells it D-a-w-g. Of Bohemian descent, I believe.

"Never heard that name, but no matter, let's move on. How old is he?"

"Dennis is 12," the Preacher replied with a straight face.

"We've never granted a doctorate to a child."

"He's a unique boy. Very mature for his age. In Tinyburg, we call him the boy preacher. Great with youth audiences. He's what you'd call a gifted student. Your distinguished school won't turn its back on a genius, would it?"

"Enough, enough!" interrupted Reverend Moss. "I know genius when I see it. Now the next question—which doctorate would Dennis prefer?"

"What kind do you offer?"

"Nearly any you can think of—for ministers, that is. Look through this booklet. If you don't find what Dennis wants, we'll make up one."

"You'd best explain these," the Preacher said, pushing the booklet back across the desk.

"Okay, let's go down the first column. To start with, let's look at our Doctor of Solicitations—that's for ministers with experience in fund-raising. And the Doctor of Empathy, for ministers who've counseled with folks in trouble. Then the Doctor of Seminars—that's for men who've gone to various workshops.

"Moving on down the list, here's a Doctor of Ecclesiology. From the Greek work *ecclesia,* meaning church. That's for ministers who've led their churches in building programs. Also the Doctor of Biblical Terminology for clergymen who've led tours to the Holy Land. Let's see, I'll skip to the Doctor of Dogmatics."

"Never heard of that one," the Preacher replied.

"That's for aggressive, persistent fellows. Anyone with dogged determination."

Remembering the doggedness of Dennis in chasing rabbits, even if he never caught any, he cried, "That's it. That's *exactly* the degree Dennis qualifies for!" There also flashed before his mind certain ministers who chase rabbits in the pulpit, jumping from topic to topic.

"Fine, fine choice!" Reverend Moss agreed in a deep, solemn voice. "Now if you'll sign here and leave your check for $50, I'll do my best to persuade my board of trustees to grant the degree."

"You mean he needn't enroll for classes or anything?"

"No, Preacher, I'm taking your word that he's eminently qualified. Now how shall we list his name on the diploma? The Reverend Dennis Dawg, Doctor of Dogmatics? Never thought how funny that sounds. But who cares? A doctor's a doctor, and every minister, if he obeys his calling, needs a doctorate."

The Preacher thanked him, wrote out the check, and said to mail the diploma to Tinyburg.

It arrived in only three days, gleaming with red ribbon and gold seal. And the lettering, in Old English, was so impressive: "The Reverend Dennis Dawg, Doctor of Dogmatics."

The Preacher enjoyed telling the story to neighboring pastors. "I'll be on vacation next month, and wonder if Dr. Dawg could preach for me?" wondered one of them. And the *Tinyburg News* actually printed a short tongue-in-cheek piece:

"Rev. Dennis Dawg, one of the most promising preacher boys in this part of the country, was awarded a Doctor of Dogmatics by the International Seminary of Pretense. Rev. Dawg—or Doctor Dawg, as he prefers to be called—is accepting a limited number of speaking engagements, so long as they don't interfere with his junior high school activities."

The following spring, the Reverend Moss hosted a testimonial dinner for former students, including Doctor Dawg.

For the dinner, Dennis wore a black wool jacket. Carol, the Preacher's wife, designed it for him. On the front, she sewed the crest of the International Seminary of Pretense. With embroidered gold letters, I.S.P., for the name of the school, it was made of dark blue felt.

Delayed by a long phone call, the Preacher, with Dennis on a leash, arrived at the dinner as the guests were finishing dessert. The Preacher led Dennis straight to the head table, pulled up two extra chairs, and ordered Dennis to hop up on one of them.

When he did, looking around at the guests as if he were one of them, his school crest sparkled for all to see. The guests assumed he was a show dog, there for after-dinner entertainment.

Reverend Moss began the program by inviting each "student" to give a testimony on, "How My Doctor's Degree Has Changed My Life." Each described his degree, such as doctor of solicitations, visitation, empathy, ecclesiology, ordinances, biblical terminology, and so on. But not one doctor of dogmatics!

As the meeting drew to an end, the Preacher asked if he might say a word:

"Distinguished and learned scholars, let me introduce one of my closest friends in the ministry, Reverend Dennis Dawg. Last fall, after strenuous study, he received his Doctor of Dogmatics at Pretense."

Snickers erupted around the room, but the Preacher continued:

"Doctor Dawg asked if he could speak, but I discouraged him. Instead, we'll do a short interview. Doctor Dawg will bark once for yes, twice for no. Everyone ready? Fine.

"Now, Doctor Dawg, is it true that your two favorite pastimes are sleeping on the back porch and chasing rabbits?"

"Arf!" barked Dennis one time, indicating the answer was yes.

"And Doctor Dawg, do I understand you earned your degree by dogged, dogmatic determination, chasing every rabbit in Tinyburg?"

"Arf!"

"Third, is it true that since you've been doctorized, you're cutting back on the number of rabbits you chase? And that you now spend more time sleeping on the back porch?"

"Arf!" (Only this time, Dennis not only barked once for yes, but wagging his tail with great excitement, look at the audience as if to say, "What a good boy am I!")

The dinner ended with restrained pandemonium. The applause was deafening, the guests still assuming Dennis was a trained show dog. The Reverend Moss, relieved that his audience thought it was entertainment, still scolded the Preacher when they got outside:

"How could you do this to me? Our records show that we gave a legitimate degree to a Reverend Dennis Dawg spelled D-a-w-g, and here you've ridiculed me by bringing in a hound dog spelled d-o-g. What do you think I'm running—a circus?"

"You said it, not me," smiled the Preacher. "But the truth is, the hound you see on the leash is the same Dennis Dawg you made a doctor out of. I have his diploma to prove it."

"But when you nominated him, you said he was a *person*, not an animal."

"You didn't ask if he were a person. You only asked if I knew any candidates for a doctorate, and when I said yes, and he has the $50, you piously said your board would 'probably' grant the degree. The truth is I hadn't left your office five minutes until your secretary had his name typed in on the diploma."

As the Preacher opened his car door and told Doctor Dawg to hop in the back seat, Reverend Moss made a final plea: "Preacher, after all I've done for you, you've made an absolute fool out of me."

"Thanks for the compliment," said the Preacher as he slipped into the driver's seat. "But you've been working on making a fool of yourself a long time. You don't need help from the likes of me and Dennis."

The Adventures of Meow-Meow

On one of the coldest nights of the winter, Mark, the Preacher's son, heard a faint "meow-meow" at the back door. It was a tiny black kitten, with white feet, who looked as if she'd been doused in water, then locked in a deep-freeze. Her fur was coated with ice, her little legs so stiff she couldn't walk.

"Mom!" Mark called, "it's a frozen cat. Can I bring her inside?"

Mark and his mother carefully wrapped her in a warm towel, then tucked her inside a carboard box, along with a hot water bottle.

"Can we keep her?" Mark asked.

"Son, I don't think she'll live. Look how listless she is."

"But cats have nine lives," he argued. "Even if she dies from the cold, she has eight more left!"

To the surprise of the whole family, the forlorn little kitten survived the night and for breakfast hungrily devoured a bowl of warm oatmeal, smothered in butter and milk. "Meow, meow," she cried, as if to say thank you.

In fact, whenever she cried, it was always "Meow, meow" two times. Never once. And never three times, such as "Meow, meow, meow." So they named her "Meow-Meow."

She preferred to stay in the warm house. And she kept close to someone all the time—hopping into Carol's lap or rubbing against the boys' legs.

The Preacher's family also noticed how Meow-Meow listened to the sound of human voices. If visitors came, she sat attentively with her ears cocked, as if she might miss something. The television also fascinated her, drawing her close like

145

a magnet. "Maybe she likes the movement on the screen, the light and shadows," Carol theorized.

But when Meow-Meow showed the same interest in the radio, they concluded she liked the voices. They were doubly certain when Meow-Meow started running to the telephone when it rang, sitting attentively, listening to both parties as if she understood every word.

"Maybe we can teach Meow-Meow to talk," joked David, another son. "Not likely," said his Dad. "She's satisfied with listening. It goes back to the cold night we saved her life. She associates our voices with that."

The Preacher has two telephones in his home—one is mounted on the kitchen wall by the refrigerator; the other sets on his desk in the den. One night at supper he cautioned everyone to be more careful in putting the receiver back, especially the one on his desk.

"Why do you say that?" asked Carol.

"Twice I've come home and found the receiver of my desk phone off the hook. Somebody's been talking, maybe went to answer the door or something, and forgot."

"Any of you guilty?" Carol asked their three sons. All shook their heads. "I've got an idea!" interrupted the Preacher. "Since Meow-Meow runs to the phone when it rings, maybe she's the one!"

"Oh, Dad, you're kidding," said Andrew. "Meow-Meow just listens—she can't pick up the phone."

Ten days later Burt David cornered the Preacher downtown: "Been trying to call you. We need to have a trustee's meeting at the church. Strange thing, when I called last Wednesday, I heard a loud noise, like someone dropped the receiver when they answered. Then what sounded like a cat crying, 'Meow, meow.' Then another 'Meow, meow.' I guess it was one of your boys, cutting up."

At supper, the Preacher raised the subject again: "Boys, do

any of you imitate a cat when you answer the phone?" Again, all three shook their heads.

"Now be honest, fellows. Something funny's going on here. First, it's the phone off the hook. Then someone imitating a cat. Yet no one knows anything about it. Our telephone's not a toy. Every day, I get church calls, most of them important. In a small town like Tinyburg, word gets around. What will people think if they keep getting busy signals because we neglect to put the receiver back, or they hear what sounds like a cat? Whoever's doing it has got to stop and I mean stop right now."

The next morning at the church, the Preacher took a call from Aunt Sarah Biggs: "Preacher, is anybody home at your house?"

"No, today is Carol's turn to help with Meals-on-Wheels and the boys are at school. Can I help you?"

"Just curious. When I dialed your house, I got an answer on the first ring. But whoever it was wouldn't say anything but 'Meow, meow.' Course I knew it wasn't no cat. But it being near April Fool's Day, I wonder if someone's tricking me."

The Preacher was speechless. Twice now, members had tried to call him at home, only to hear a silly "Meow, meow." He'd read about hackers who pry into computers. *I wonder,* he mused, *if someone's tapped into our line and doing this to embarrass me?*

He reached to call the telephone office, then decided this could make him look sillier. So he put it off. "If it happens a third time," he mused, "we'll change our number, maybe try an unlisted number for a while."

The mystery, however, was solved quicker than he dreamed. That evening, Carol greeted him with a "You won't believe this!" kind of story: "I was taking a nap when the phone rang. I was slow answering, and before I did, the cat bounded up on your desk, nudged the receiver off the hook with her nose, cried 'Meow, meow' two times, then cocked her ears to listen!"

"Carol, do you expect me to believe that? No cat knows enough to answer a telephone."

"Most cats don't, but Meow-Meow loves to hear people talk and will do anything to listen in. Besides, I saw her with my own eyes."

"Let's test it," he said. "You run over to the church, dial our number. I'll let it ring and see what happens." What happened is what Carol had reported—Meow-Meow bounded to the phone on the first ring and nudged the receiver off the hook!

Aunt Sarah grinned when the Preacher told her. And being a fun-loving person, she decided to have a little merriment of her own. So she asked to see the Preacher in his office, saying she needed counseling for a problem.

"Now tell me exactly what's bothering you, Aunt Sarah," the Preacher began on the afternoon of her appointment.

"It's this way," she began, tongue in cheek. "Your family likes cats. Too much, I say. Even hired a cat to answer your phone. As you know, I take pride in being a Bible scholar. I've searched and searched my concordance, but nowhere in the Good Book can you find the word *cat*. Not one cat in the whole Bible.

"Now if God wanted us to make cats part of the family, answer phones and all that, wouldn't He have mentioned them at least one time?

"The Bible describes other animals: dogs, camels, bulls, deer, fox, goats, horses, hyenas, jackals, sheep, lions, leopards, oxen, mice, swine, weasels, and even wolves. But not one verse in all the 66 books of the Bible will you find a single cat mentioned."

Until this point Aunt Sarah kept a straight face. But now she broke into convulsive laughter, which relieved the Preacher, for at first he wondered if she were serious.

Well—as the Preacher predicted—in a place like Tinyburg, population 1,473, word gets around. And soon it was common knowledge that calls to the pastorium were likely to be answered by a cat, which—in the eyes of at least one church member—was unscriptural!

The Preacher's family blamed Meow-Meow for their growing number of phone calls. "Some of our friends call just to hear Meow-Meow," reported Andrew. "Say Dad, let's ask for a new number, one that spells something."

"Spells something like what?" his Dad asked.

"If no one in Tinyburg has the number 228-2255, let's ask if they'll assign it to us."

"Why?"

"Because 228-2255 spells the words CAT CALL, easy for anyone to remember."

"You're a bright boy," replied his Dad, "but bright in the wrong way. We're getting all the cat calls we need. Tomorrow, I'm replacing my desk phone with one mounted on the wall. More trouble to answer, but it'll be safe from Meow-Meow."

So, sadly, Meow-Meow never got to answer the phone again. But regardless of when the phone rings—during her nap or in the middle of a snack—she bounds to its side, straining to hear the words!

Sunday evening services at the Tinyburg Church are informal, often with a folksy approach. So three months later, after most members had forgotten the cat episode, the Preacher decided to give a tongue-in-cheek devotional talk. He did so mainly for Aunt Sarah's sake. He needed to even the score. And he knew Aunt Sarah's sense of humor gave him the freedom to do so.

Accordingly, on a Sunday night in August, with as straight a face as possible, he began his devotional talk. Aunt Sarah, as usual, sat near the front, pencil in hand, ready to make notes. Only tonight she sat spellbound, too intrigued to write anything. Here, condensed, is what the Preacher said:

"Although the Bible's a great and noble book, many good and helpful topics are not mentioned. The Bible is truth, but it makes no claim to cover the whole range of human knowledge.

"For example, the Bible makes no mention of cats (to which Aunt Sarah nodded), penicillin, Interstate highways, airplanes, or television. The Bible is silent on such subjects as zip codes, telephones, radio, Dairy Queen, computers, daily newspapers, Mother's Day, Halloween, vitamins, country music, or baseball. For that matter, it completely omits Tinyburg, the United States, the World Series, the Rose Bowl parade, President Ronald Reagan, Pepsi-Cola, Will Rogers, and microwave ovens.

"The list of what the Bible leaves out is almost endless. But my emphasis tonight is on cats. Some say they have nine lives. Others claim that when the cat's away, the mice do play, and that a gloved cat catches no mice. I like the nursery rhyme:

> Pussy cat, pussy cat, where have you been?
> I've been to London to see the queen.
> Pussy cat, pussy cat, what did you there?
> I frightened a little mouse under the chair.

"In that simple verse, I see a profound truth, not likely intended by the author. This country cat—whatever her name— got a chance to visit the big city of London, even the palace of the Queen of England. While there, she could have met famous people, visited historic sites. Instead, she busied herself with chasing a mouse under the chair where the Queen sat.

"Back home with her country cousins, all she could report on was that she chased a mouse—something she could have done in any corn crib on the farm.

"Beloved, although the Bible's silent on the subject of cats, we're close to the message of the Bible when we say that some people waste their time on trivial pursuits, while others seek for noble and lasting ways to invest their lives."

Aunt Sarah joked as she shook hands at the door: "Preacher, here's another topic for a sermon. You say Interstate highways aren't in the Bible, and I agree. So next Sunday, give us a sermon, say, on 'How to Get to Heaven When You Can't Take the Interstate!'"

"OK," he agreed, "as long as you work up a talk on, 'How to Cook Dinner in Heaven Without a Microwave Oven.'"

"It's a deal," she said, "if you'll enroll Meow-Meow in my ladies Sunday School class!"

Casper the Parrot

At least every other summer, Candice Spiller makes a trip overseas and always brings back something for the Tinyburg Church. From a vacation trip to Switzerland, she brought home a lovely hand-embroidered table cloth which the ladies use when they serve tea in the new church parlor. On a trip to Israel, she brought a beautiful set of olive-wood candle holders which the church uses during the communion services. From Germany she brought a hand-carved, miniature manger scene which is displayed each Christmas in the church foyer.

Although the members assumed Candice would bring something from her trip to Panama, they were surprised when she came home to Tinyburg with a live parrot. He was a beautiful bird with a green body, yellow head, and brilliant tail feathers of blue, green, and scarlet.

"His name is Casper, and I'm giving him to the children's department in Sunday School," Candice announced with pride. "Casper can boost attendance because the children will look forward to seeing him each Sunday, teaching him new words, and bringing him nuts and seeds to eat."

Candice got home that summer in time to direct the Vacation Bible School. For publicity, she designed gaily decorated posters, using the colors of blue, green, and yellow to match Casper's feathers.

> Come one, come all
> to Bible School.
> See Casper, parrot!
> Listen to him talk,
> Teach him new words!
> 8:30 AM daily.

Uncle Billy Cutrell was finishing a late breakfast in the Tinyburg Cafe the morning Candice came in to ask permission to put one of her posters in the front window. Her father, Clay Barker, president of the Tinyburg Realty Company, happened to be there at the same time.

As soon as Candice left, Uncle Billy said to Clay, "I can appreciate that nativity set your daughter brought from Germany, but when it comes to donating live animals such as birds to a church, that's going too far."

Clay, taking up for his daughter, reminded Uncle Billy that a bird's not exactly an animal, and, besides, Casper could say "I love Jesus" in Spanish.

"I don't care if he can say the whole Ten Commandments in Latin, a church is not a zoo," Uncle Billy shot back. "What if someone decides to give the church one of those man-eating pythons, or maybe a crocodile, would you accept that?"

"Uncle Billy, don't be foolish. All we've got here is a harmless, little feathered bird. You're being ridiculous to compare Casper to a crocodile."

But Uncle Billy wasn't satisfied to drop the subject. "Another thing," he reminded Clay. "I was reading the other day that some parrots live to be as much as sixty years old. If the church accepts that parrot, we're obligating ourselves to feed and take care of it for years on end. Next thing you know, someone will suggest we retire it to a nursing shelter for aged pets, and you know what that could cost the church!"

Clay Barker drew a big sigh, laid a fifteen-cent tip on the table for his $3.75 "all-you-can-eat" breakfast and headed for the door. Regardless, Clay knew that Uncle Billy would have the last word, and he had no more time to prolong the argument. A ten o'clock appointment with a buyer for the biggest farm in the county was more important than all the parrots in South America.

Sure enough, Uncle Billy was not satisfied to drop the matter. Retired from the Tinyburg street department, Uncle Billy has time to think matters through, to consider all angles of a problem—something that fellows such as Clay Barker don't have.

So at the next church business meeting, Uncle Billy raised the question again. "I think it's time for the church to reconsider its policy about accepting any donations other than money," he began. "Before you know it, our beautiful church here could look like a combination junkyard and wildlife preserve. We've got a Properties Committee. I suggest we ask them to make a study. Until we decide, let's ask Candice to keep Casper at her house where he belongs."

"And another thing," he continued. "You claim Casper can speak Spanish, and supposedly says, 'I love Jesus.' Well, I listened to that bird the other afternoon, and for all I know, he's saying bad words. Now imagine our little kiddies coming here to Bible School in a few weeks, all excited about a parrot, and unbeknownst to them, listening to bad words in a foreign language. It's a risk we don't need. It's a disgrace. Children hear enough on television these days: they don't need to learn profanity from parrots in churches."

Since Uncle Billy was so concerned, the church asked him to meet with the Properties Committee.

Several proposals were made. They included: refusing the gift altogether, giving Casper to the Tinyburg children's zoo, cutting out his tongue so he wouldn't disturb services, and offering him as a prize to the youngster who brought the most new members to Bible School.

But there were objections. The committee chairman reminded them that if they gave the parrot back to Candice, this would offend her. In turn, she and her family as well as her parents, Mr. and Mrs. Barker, might leave the church and start going to Bigtown. "Lot more's at stake here than just a parrot," he reminded the committee, and looked straight at Uncle Billy.

After a two-hour discussion, the committee reached a compromise to which Uncle Billy agreed. First, in the future, all proposed gifts to the church in the form of tangible property, birds, or animals first be approved by the Properties Committee. And second, the church would accept Casper, the parrot, on a trial basis, at least until after Vacation Bible School.

The reasoning was that the posters all over town had already told about Casper, and it would be unfair to disappoint the children who came to Bible School. Uncle Billy won two final concessions before the committee adjourned. First, on Sundays, the parrot's cage would be covered with a heavy, black velvet cloth. And second, the Spanish teacher at the Tinyburg high school would verify that Casper was saying "I love Jesus" in Spanish.

With the problem settled, at least for now, Candice turned her attention to the Bible school. An avid promoter, she and some of the other church ladies for several summers had invited children of some of the migrant workers to send their children to Bible School.

Each summer about the time for Bible School, a dozen or so Mexican families arrived to pick apples in a nearby orchard. But the children felt strange, and only one or two had ever come. Some didn't speak English well, and this added to their embarrassment.

This summer, Candice had a novel idea. Why not take Casper when she visited the migrant camp? Listening to Casper say "I love Jesus" in Spanish might win their confidence.

If ever Candice Spiller had a brilliant idea, this was it!— even more brilliant than the year she rented a camel from a traveling circus to appear in the church Christmas pageant.

When Candice arrived at the migrant camp, she went door to door to the cottages, asking the children to meet her outside. When a crowd gathered, she took Casper out of his cage and let him sit on her sleeve.

"Good morning, Casper," she said to him. "These children

are your friends. They want to attend Bible School at the Tinyburg Church where they can see you every morning. Can you say something to them?"

By now, even the smallest of the children, who had hidden timidly behind their older brothers and sisters, were crowding up close.

Casper crooked his neck and, with a friendly look in his eyes, said: "*Yo amo a Jesús, Yo amo a Jesús, Yo amo a Jesús.*"

By now, the children were joining Casper like a chorus, "*Yo amo a Jesús, Yo amo a Jesús, Yo amo a Jesús!*"

When Bible School opened the next Monday morning, it seemed that every youngster from the migrant camp was present. Some of the teachers, running short of materials for crafts, wondered if Candice was too successful in her publicity.

But everyone had a wonderful time and by week's end, the Mexican children felt as much at home in the Tinyburg Church as those who had come all their lives.

Since the children were so fascinated by Casper's ability to say: "I love Jesus," Candice suggested they learn the chorus "Oh, How I Love Jesus" to sing at commencement.

Moreover, one of the high school girls who was helping and had studied Spanish for two years, translated the words into Spanish. This fascinated the local youngsters who quickly caught on to the words. So, every day, they joined in the chorous, singing first in English, then in Spanish. And at the end, on signal from Candice, Casper chirped, "I love Jesus, too." You see, Candice had taught him the extra word *t-o-o* or *también* in Spanish.

When announcements went out to the parents for the commencement night, Candice mentioned that Casper would give a part of the program, too.

Naturally, the church was filled, including a number of the Mexican parents from the apple orchards.

The program climaxed when the children gathered at the front of the church and sang, first in English:

Oh, how I love Jesus,
Oh, how I love Jesus,
Oh, how I love Jesus,
Because He first loved me.
FREDERICK WHITFIELD

Then they sang in Spanish:

Oh, cuanto le amo
Oh, cuanto le amo
Oh, cuanto le amo
Jesús murió por mí.

And right on cue, Casper spoke up, *"Yo amo a Jesús también, Yo amo a Jesús también, Yo amo a Jesús también!"*
This really brought the house down. The timing was unbelievable. Even more unbelievable was the look in Casper's eyes which were fixed right on Uncle Billy, as if to say, "How do you like that, mister?"

"I'll hand it to you, Candice," Uncle Billy greeted her after the benediction. "You touched this old heart of mine like it's not been touched in a long time. How those little Mexican children sang! I could listen all night. Made me think of that Bible verse from Psalms 8:2, 'Out of the mouth of babes and sucklings hast thou ordained strength.' Only tonight, the good Lord used the tongue of a parrot, too!"

The members of Tinyburg Church never had to decide the destiny of Casper. Candice saw to that.

"I've had second thoughts about Casper," she told the Properties Committee. "It wouldn't be fair to Casper to leave him in a church building all week, with no one around. Parrots enjoy being with other people, so I've decided to give him to the Tinyburg children's zoo.

"However, the zoo keeper promised me that we can borrow Casper each summer for Bible School."

The committee agreed this was a good idea, so the next morning, Candice delivered Casper to his new home.

Whenever you visit Tinyburg, stop by the children's zoo and say hello to Casper. Or, if it's during Bible School, you can see him in church. He still speaks in Spanish and enjoys greeting all his friends with the five words *Yo amo a Jesús también*, which mean, "I love Jesus, too."

Fluffie's First Communion

For generations, little children have enjoyed playing church, especially those who live in small towns and rural areas. They use their imaginations for play-like weddings, funerals, and summer revivals. They also make games out of baptizings, choir practices, and old-time homecomings with dinner on the ground.

This kind of religious make-believe goes back at least 2,000 years, to Jesus' day. Luke 7:1-32 quotes Jesus about children of His day playing wedding and funeral.

As you might expect, youngsters in Tinyburg enjoy playing church, too, especially Mark and Andrew (the Preacher's sons), and Rhonda and Ruthie (the daughters of Ted and Candice Spiller).

Oh, sometimes they enlist the help of Fluffie, a mixed-breed, grayish-white kitten who belongs to Ruthie and Rhonda. Docile and obliging, Fluffie's been baptized enough times to make her a member of every church in Tinyburg, as well as Bigtown.

The first time these four kids played communion, they argued over what to serve. A bite of something representative of Jesus' body was no problem—they crumbled up bits of Ritz crackers which they served on an aluminum pie pan, the disposable kind. And they used little Dixie cups for the communion wine, although it wasn't actually wine.

Mark, however, insisted on real wine: "My best friend at school goes to a church that serves wine, and I think we should, too."

"No," argued Rhonda. "Wine could make us drunk!"

"Just a little sip?" wondered Mark.

"OK, smartie, where would you get some wine?"

"Where will you get real grape juice?" argued Andrew, siding with his brother in a plea for the fermented kind.

"Easy," replied Ruthie. "Each month, our daddy buys a big bottle of Welch's grape juice for communion. He and Mother set the communion table and pour the grape juice into tiny cups. Daddy is so saving that he keeps a little funnel in the church kitchen, to pour the leftover juice back in the bottle."

"Could us kids drink some of it?" replied Mark.

"Sure—just go over to the church kitchen and look in the refrigerator."

Since Andrew was the oldest, the other three volunteered him to run to the church for the leftover bottle of grape juice.

"What if we drink it all, and your daddy finds out?" inquired Andrew. The sisters shrugged their shoulders, which told Andrew that four Dixie cups of the juice wouldn't be missed.

While Andrew was fetching the Welch grape juice, the girls spread a cover across an orange crate and Mark ran home to see if any birthday candles were left from his mother's party last week.

"Mark, you know I don't want you playing with matches," scolded his mother, Carol, when she found him pilfering in the kitchen cabinets.

"It's only a party under the trees," he explained. "I need to light a couple of candles, not start a bonfire."

By the time Mark returned with the candles, Andrew had the bottle of grape juice and the make-believe communion table was ready to be set.

Just as Andrew finished filling the tiny cups, Rhonda let out a cry:

"Oh, this is terrible, this is horrible! I just realized this grape juice is poison. If we drink it, we'll all die and go down to the bad place."

"Bad place?" mocked Andrew. "Taking communion makes

you better. Daddy preaches that if a person takes it serious, communion brings him close to God, not further away."

"But you don't understand," pled Rhonda. "This isn't like ordinary juice at the grocery. Your Daddy blessed this juice, every drop, when he held it up last Sunday and prayed. Drinking it now isn't like drinking it in church. I'm afraid to drink one drop. God might strike me dead."

"I'm not afraid to drink the whole bottle," mocked Andrew, holding it to his lips.

"Stop, silly!" screamed Rhonda. "You'll die and we can never play communion again, and we'll all have to go to a real funeral, and I'll cry when they sing those sad songs over your casket, and I'll never, never, never get to play church again."

Realizing Rhonda was serious, the boys asked if she had a better idea.

"I do now!" she squealed after a moment's thought. "Grape Kool-Aid—we've got a hunded zillion packages at home. I'll run and get one, then we can drink all we please."

"Kool-Aid's OK," Andrew cried after her. "But when you play communion, you don't make a pig of yourself. You only take a sip."

So off she scampered for a package of Kool-Aid. "And remember some water and a pitcher to mix it in," Ruthie cried after her.

While Rhonda was gone, Mark spoke up, "I wish we had a bigger crowd. When we take communion at church, Daddy encourages everyone to come."

"You mean invite the whole town?" wondered Ruthie.

"Course not. Maybe one or two more, besides us."

"Like who?" Ruthie asked in a skeptical voice.

"I know," cried Mark as he jumped around on one foot, the way he does when he learns he's going to a circus or something. "We'll invite Fluffie! Remember how we baptized her the last time we played church?"

"Serve communion to a cat?" Ruthie replied in a holierthan-thou tone. "Cats don't take communion—they don't even go to Sunday School!"

"OK, Miss-Know-It-All," answered Andrew. "Why did you let her be baptized? You begged your Mom to make her a little baptismal robe out of an old pillow case. At real church, Daddy says communion is for baptized Christians."

"Fluffie's baptized—but she's no Christian," argued Ruthie.

"Well, she's half a Christian, for you helped baptize her," joined in Andrew. "And I think she's just as good a church member as you."

By now, Rhonda was back with the grape Kool-Aid, which she and Ruthie mixed in a pitcher.

"Rhonda," whispered Ruthie, "the boys want to invite Fluffie to communion. What do you think?"

"I think it's great," Rhonda answered, loud enough for the neighborhood to hear. "And since I got the Kool-Aid, it's your turn to find Fluffie. And this being her first communion, bring her little baptismal robe that Mother made and let her wear it again."

Fortunately, it was a long, summer afternoon, or they'd have run out of time preparing everything—the candles, the Ritz crackers, the Dixie cups of grape juice, and Fluffie, dressed in her white robe.

It was Mark's turn to offer the prayer, saying something like, "Jesus, this may be Kool-Aid, but it's the best we can do. Thank You for it. And thanks, too, for orange and strawberry Kool-Aid, but we'll never serve that at communion. Amen. And oh, yes, bless Fluffie, since this is her first communion."

This brought on another crisis, for Fluffie refused to drink the Kool-Aid. "Hold her mouth open and pour it down anyway," advised Mark. "That's the way Daddy gives worm pills to our dog."

"But Fluffie's no dog, and Kool-Aid's not for worms," scolded Rhonda. "Mark, you say the silliest things. This is supposed to be religious."

"But if she doesn't drink, she won't get blessed," argued Mark. "We've got to find something she'll drink, or Fluffie will be a heathen the rest of her life! Got any ideas?"

"Milk," answered Ruthie and Rhonda, almost in unison. "She won't drink anything else, even Pepsi-Cola."

"I know a way to make her drink," shot back Andrew. "We've got some leftover Easter egg dye, a purple color. Let's mix Fluffie a little cup of milk, you know, make it purple, like grape juice. She'll never know."

So that's how Fluffie was led by Mark and Andrew, Ruthie and Rhonda, to observe her first communion. She even licked her whiskers of every drop, unconcerned that for the first time in her life she was drinking purple milk—milk that was supposed to be grape juice, blessed with good intentions, if not with divine approval.

A few Sundays later when real communion was served in the Tinyburg Church, Mark and Andrew listened quietly as their daddy read: "And as they were eating, Jesus took bread, and blessed it, and brake it . . . and said, Take, eat; this is my body. And he took the cup, and gave thanks . . . saying, Drink ye all of it; For this is my blood of the new testament, which is shed for many for the remission of sins" (Matt. 26:26-28).

And under their breath, the boys prayed, "And Lord, if you didn't mean those Bible verses for cats, too, don't take it out on Fluffie. We made her do it!"

Uncle Billy Renews His Driver's License

Shortly before his seventy-fifth birthday, Uncle Billy Cutrell received a notice to renew his driver's license: "Dear Mr. Cutrell: Now that you have reached seventy-five, you must take an annual road test. Please bring this notice within thirty days for your test."

Uncle Billy, who takes pride in his unblemished driving record, flinched at the notice, but accepted it as inevitable: "Naturally, many so-called drivers, at age seventy-five, who've lost their vigor and manhood, shouldn't be allowed on the highways. So I won't complain, although in my case it's a routine test."

Senior Citizens Day was the following Sunday in the Tinyburg Church. In his message, the Preacher warned his senior members that ageism is as bad as sexism or racism: "Stand up for your rights! And watch for put-downs. Scrutinize the ads you see on television. Boycott businesses that ridicule older people."

Uncle Billy, who never remembered hearing the word *ageism*, took it to heart, determined to watch for it in advertising.

He didn't wait long, for that afternoon a TV commercial for automatic washers featured an ecstatic great-grandmother. She was excited over her new washer because the controls were so simple. Then turning to her aged husband, who was leaned back in his rocking chair with an out-of-this-world look on his face, she winked at the camera, "Even old Grandad might learn to use this model!"

Uncle Billy saw the ad for what it was—a put-down on elderly men, absent-mindedly rocking away the hours, unable to distinguish the "On" and "Off" switches on a washing machine. The ad was still on his mind as he drove to Bigtown the next morning to renew his license.

"Good morning, young man!" greeted a thirty-year-old clerk behind the desk. Uncle Billy, putting on his best act, turned around to see who the "young man" was.

"Oh, I'm sorry," the clerk explained, "I was talking to you!"

"Sorry for what?" bristled Uncle Billy. "Sorry I'm old? Sorry you called me the opposite of what I am?"

The clerk, realizing he had put his foot in the mouth, apologized: "I was only trying to cheer you up. Bring your renewal notice?"

Uncle Billy, undeterred, stayed on the subject: "When you say you want to make me feel good, are you insinuating I don't feel good, just because I'm seventy-five? Can't you accept me for what I am—must you try to flatter me, make me something I'm not. Well listen, Mr. Smart Britches, I'm not a young man, and I don't want you calling me young any more than you want me to ask, 'How are you feeling, *old* man?' Would you call a man a woman, or a woman a man, just to make them 'feel better'?"

The young clerk, who was new on the job anyway and didn't want his superiors to overhear an argument with a seventy-five-year-old man, changed the subject: "Now for the road test. It's required, you know, of drivers over seventy-five?"

"Yes, I know," Uncle Billy replied. "I suppose, however, that if I'd gone along with this 'Good morning, young man!' I could have avoided the test."

"Is your car outside?" the clerk asked, cryptically. "This won't take long." And it didn't. The clerk was so anxious to quieten Uncle Billy that he asked him to drive around the block just one time, and skipped such tests as backing into a tight parking spot and parking on an incline.

Back inside, the clerk smiled, "You did well, Mr. Cutrell. Now all you need to do is pose while I make an instamatic photo for your new license."

"Changed my mind," Uncle Billy replied, tongue in cheek. "I need to think this over. Maybe I'm too old to drive. My license's good for another ten days. I'll come back next week."

The clerk, fearful he had offended Uncle Billy and that he might make a complaint to the state agency that employed him, urged Uncle Billy to go ahead now, rather than having to take the driver's test over. "The next examiner might be tougher and turn you down," he warned.

"Toughness don't bother me none," Uncle Billy replied. "What I'm looking for is a teeny little bit of courtesy, the kind we once had a lot of!"

Driving back to Tinyburg, Uncle Billy rehearsed the episode in his mind. Always a practical joker, and with little else to do, he decided to give the license examiner something to remember. Here's how.

The same evening, he called on Candice Spiller to ask if she had any make-up from last year's Christmas pageant. Candice, who majored in drama in college, is widely known for her successful pageants, which she directs each Christmas.

"Yes," she replied, "but I'm saving everything for next Christmas."

"In that case," Uncle Billy said with a sly smile in his eye, "let's play like it's Christmas right now."

"How's that?"

"If you've got a man's wig of coal-black hair and the right kind of theatrical make-up, I want you to change me into a dashing, thirty-year-old!"

Candice, thinking it must be some kind of joke, hardly knew what to say.

"I'm as serious as a bride's mother at the altar," he answered. "If you need more pancake makeup, or youthful clothing that will fit me, I'll pay what it costs. Believe you me, I'm going on a spree that will make headlines!" And he did, with the help of Candice Spiller who each December can make ten-year-old boys look like seventy-year-old Wise Men from the East.

The result was that three mornings later Uncle Billy showed up at the license office wearing a wig of wavy black hair, a checked sportcoat borrowed from Candice's teenage son, and clip-on sun glasses. With expert deftness, Candice had applied makeup to cover all his wrinkles. He suddenly lost forty-five years off his appearance!

"Good morning," the clerk greeted him warmly. "Nice day out there. What can we do for you?"

When Uncle Billy showed his renewal notice, the clerk, with a puzzled look, noted that another applicant from Tinyburg with the same name had been there earlier in the week.

"Same name, same man," Uncle Billy explained.

"Couldn't be—he was more than twice your age. Lots of wrinkles, hardly any hair. But something's fishy about both of you, for this application says you're seventy-five!"

"Young man," Uncle Billy proceeded, "just what is a seventy-five-year-old man supposed to look like? Are you an expert in guessing ages? Can you prove I'm not seventy-five? Do you have a secret diagram of what a given person looks like? If so, draw me the specifications."

The clerk, recalling the hassel with the other William Cutrell, wondered if he was headed down another dead-end street. *I can't imagine what kind of people live in Tinyburg,* he whispered under his breath.

So he continued: "You need a driver's license, right? I'm sorry I got off the subject. But Mr. Cutrell, there's no way I can renew your license and take a picture of you and state that you're seventy-five. If you're stopped for a traffic violation and the officer compares your picture with your age, he'll know somebody goofed. And I could be charged with issuing a license to the wrong person. Your age, and the photo I make, have got to come out pretty even."

"Then you can't renew my license?"

"I can't afford to get you—or myself—into trouble. As I said, the age and the face have got to match, at least half-way. Your face looks thirty, your application says seventy-five."

"Then you're an authority on how people should look?" Uncle Billy asked, but getting no answer. "Then I'll think it over and come back later."

But instead of returning to Tinyburg, he stopped at the *Bigtown Bugle* where he told his story to the city editor.

Sensing the potential for human interest, the editor asked for more details, then printed this story in the next edition:

Senior Citizen Denied License
Because of Youthful Appearance

Alongside the article were two pictures of Uncle Billy with the caption, "Will the real Mr. Cutrell please stand up?" One photo showed him made up as a thirty-year-old with the cut-line, Bill Cutrell. The other, as he is in real life, was identified as William J. Cutrell. The entire article was tongue-in-cheek, but when his friends in Tinyburg saw it, Uncle Billy became an instant celebrity.

No more than two hours after the papers hit the streets, the licensing office called Uncle Billy: "Mr. Cutrell—could you come in for your driver's test today? Dress anyway you please; no questions asked."

Well, Uncle Billy is enough of a clown that he again asked Candice to dress him as a thirty-year-old. And wearing his wig and checkered sport coat, he returned to Bigtown to renew his license. This time, the clerk snapped his photo without comment.

For a whole year, Uncle Billy continued to be a celebrity in Tinyburg, friends begging to see his driver's license and photo. Fortunately, no law official ever asked to see it, so there was no problem explaining the age on the license compared with his youthful picture.

A year later, when he returned for his annual road test, Uncle Billy left the wig and make-up at home. The clerk greeted him as he would anyone else: "Good morning, Mr. Cutrell. What can we do for you, sir?"

And Uncle Billy liked that, for it reminded him of Tinyburg—where all the boys and girls say "Yes, Sir" and "No, Sir" and "Yes, M'am" and "No, M'am" whether you're thirty or whether you're seventy-five!

Squeakie Moves to Tinyburg

Squeakie is the name of a church mouse who lives in the Bigtown Church in Bigtown. As you probably know, you can find at least one church mouse in every church regardless of size. Squeakie's wife is named Sweetie, and their little boy mouse is Tweetie. So there we have the three of them: Squeakie, Sweetie, and Tweetie. Each has grey fur, tiny whiskers, and bright, beady eyes.

Regardless of weather, they're always at church. And they never take vacations. Even when sickness strikes, they are present.

Each has his assigned listening post. Sweetie, the mother mouse, takes in choir practice, the church nursery, and the women's meetings. Squeakie, the daddy mouse, eavesdrops on telephone calls, goes to board and deacon meetings, and listens carefully to any conversations in the hallways and in the pews. Tweetie, the boy mouse, covers the youth activities, keeps an eye on the church custodian, and attends all social events such as Christmas parties, baby showers, and picnics.

At least once a week, the three get together to share their notes. Oh, they don't actually keep notebooks, but their memory is so good they can repeat most everything they hear. Squeakie and his wife often confide in each other that they know more about what goes on in the Bigtown Church than does the minister whose name is the Reverend Henry Moss, D.D.

It's not that they're nosy and enjoy picking up church gossip. What they listen for is announcements of church suppers or plans to install new mouse traps. As Squeakie said one night when they were licking crumbs from a potluck dinner,

"There's no better living for a mouse than to find himself a good church home. Tweetie, when you grow up, I hope you won't settle for a private home or a even a commercial building such as a store or office suite. True, department stores sell all kinds of goodies such as cookies and candies. But you can't improve on the menu at a church supper. I don't care where you go."

With that remark, Squeakie helped himself to another crumb of homemade coconut layer cake, one of his favorite delicacies. Fact is, Squeakie knows the Bigtown Church member who bakes the best coconut cakes, and he's disappointed if she misses a potluck.

"Pop, I apologize for bringing up an unpleasant subject while we're enjoying this good food, but last night I heard some horrifying news at a meeting of the building and grounds committee."

"How's that?" asked his mother, Sweetie.

"The committee voted to employ a pest exterminator. He promised the committee he could rid the entire church of mice in seven days."

"Whoever heard of driving out all the mice from as big a church as this in just one week?" Squeakie asked, without a trace of worry in his voice.

"He's going to use what he calls poison and deadly bait. Said mice just gobble it up."

"Oh dear," Sweetie said, as she dropped a morsel of coconut on the floor. "This means the end of our happy home. Why could anyone, especially church people, be so cruel? Squeakie, I don't see how you can be so unconcerned."

"Sweetie, the reason I'm not worried is that I already decided this church has gotten too big for us. I can no longer keep up with all the new faces we see every Sunday. We need to find a smaller church, where you know everyone. Besides, it's getting to where there are too many committees and activities. We hardly have an evening to ourselves. Another good thing, most smaller churches can't afford an extermination service. They depend on mouse traps and the like. After we drew a map of the church here and pinpointed the traps, we found it easy to detour around them. We can do the same wherever we move."

When Tweetie wondered how they would choose a new church home, Squeakie reminded him to keep his eyes and ears open. "Maybe a new member will transfer here from a smaller church. He's sure to give the address of his old church to the office secretary, maybe describe what it was like. Another thing, the Bigtown pastor receives at least a hundred bulletins from other churches. You know how he keeps up with the smaller churches, playing as if he were sort of a bishop, handpicking their pastors, and the like. Once he tosses those bulletins in his wastebasket, we'll fish them out, then take turns reading. We're bound to get several leads."

As it turned out, they didn't have to depend on bulletins from other churches. Instead, the following afternoon, Sweetie heard the most amazing announcement at the women's mission society which met in the parlor. Sweetie, hiding inside a centerpiece of flowers, could hardly wait to tell Squeakie and Tweetie.

"It's the best news ever," she announced at bedtime. "The ladies voted to collect used clothing to send to a church in what they call Tinyburg. It's not far from Bigtown, thirty-five miles I believe. That's a long way on foot, but maybe we can find transportation if we decide to move."

Squeakie, stroking his whiskers, asked if the ladies shared any details about Tinyburg.

"Oh yes, seems the population is 1,473. They said it's a place where the air's pure and clean, and everyone sleeps well at night, just like the Sominex ads say."

"What's Sominex?" Tweetie wondered.

"I haven't the slightest idea, but let me finish. They said the Tinyburg Church is a friendly little congregation, but doesn't have a big modern building. No youth program to speak of. Major on the Sunday services with little going on during the week. Sounds like a perfect setup to me, for there wouldn't be nearly the committee meetings to attend."

"What about potluck suppers?" wondered Tweetie. "We'll miss our good eats here at Bigtown."

"Never worry," interrupted Squeakie. "I grew up in a small church. In fact, that's where your mother and I met. Did a lot of our courting at church socials, ice-cream suppers, and Halloween parties. Fabulous foods. In fact, smaller churches can outdo the bigger ones when it comes to home cooking."

"Can we move to Tinyburg tonight?" Tweetie asked, his little boy whiskers moving up and down like windshield wipers.

"I wish we could," Squeakie replied, "for that exterminator man could come any day. But we've got to find some transportation. By the way, did the ladies say how they'll pack the used clothing?"

"It's all worked out," Sweetie explained. "They're putting three big collection boxes in the hall. Members have until next Monday to bring their donations. That afternoon, a committee will seal the boxes and arrange for a United Parcel truck to pick them up."

"A United Parcel truck coming right here to the church?" interrupted Squeakie.

"Of course, where else would it come?"

"Sweetie, we've just got us free, one-way tickets to Tinyburg. We'll hide in the bottom of those boxes, one to each box. We need to be in there not later than, say, three o'clock Monday afternoon. If possible, burrow down into a child's sock. Makes good insulation if the weather's cold. Also, no one can see us. Sweetie, can you pack each of us a sack lunch? Once the boxes are unloaded at Tinyburg, we can gnaw ourselves out, find sleeping quarters, and set up housekeeping before anyone dreams we're on the place."

"Horray for Tinyburg!" shouted Tweetie. "Hooray for the

UPS truck! Horray for the ice-cream suppers and Halloween candy."

"Shh," warned Sweetie. "This must be a secret."

Had you watched carefully the following Monday afternoon, you would have seen, one at a time, three mice scurry down the main hall of the Bigtown Church, each lugging a tremendous traveling bag. With great effort, each hoisted himself over the side of one of the clothing boxes, then quickly disappeared in a deep corner of soft clothing. "Just like an overnight camping trip," Tweetie told himself.

Not long after, a committee of women sealed the boxes and wrote in big letters across the top of each: "Tinyburg Church in Tinyburg, seven miles south of Pretense. Rush, fragile, do not drop."

Although the contents of the boxes weren't fragile, the three mice were still glad they wrote this warning, hoping it would mean a smoother and safer ride.

I have no regrets leaving Bigtown, Sweetie said to herself as the big truck pulled out of town and headed south toward Tinyburg. "Now I won't worry about exterminators and watching everything that Tweetie eats."

Within an hour, all three mice overheard the driver as he read aloud from a giant billboard:

Welcome to Tinyburg: the only city in the United States with an unlisted zip code!

Since it was still daylight when the driver unloaded the three boxes at the Tinyburg Church, the three mice waited until after dark to start gnawing their way to freedom.

"I can see why they call it Tinyburg," Tweetie remarked, looking over the small church sanctuary. "This isn't big enough to hold the choir of the Bigtown Church."

"That's all right," explained Squeakie. "The Bigtown Church was getting too big for us to cover—too many meetings to attend, too much going on. Here we can take it easier."

"Regardless of size, we still must eat," interrupted Sweetie, the mother mouse. "Tweetie, your job is to learn when they have their church suppers. No need of me fixing meals when we can enjoy our share of those nice potlucks. Also scout around the nursery as churches often keep crackers and cookies for the little ones."

They felt so lucky when Tweetie heard there would be an all-church supper on Friday night. "They'll be bringing in some of the food on Thursday," Sweetie predicted. "So Tweetie, keep an eye open. We can start sampling even before the food's put on the tables."

Thursday morning, Pearl Ramsey came lugging into the church kitchen four half-gallon, home-canned jars of cherries which she'd brought to Tinyburg when they moved from the farm. Within minutes, she was mixing up three, big cherry cobblers which she baked in flat pans. Tweetie looked on in wonder. Never had he seen, or smelled, anything like it—homemade cherry cobblers, the juice bubbling and running over the sides. He could hardly wait for Pearl to leave, so he could taste a sample.

What Tweetie didn't know was how long it takes a big cobbler to cool off. So when he gingerly felt his way along the edge of the big baking pans, he accidently slipped on some of the syrup, and one foot fell into the still-warm cobbler. In fact, it was so hot that he burned himself, scurrying to his mother, whimpering. His mother quickly licked off the hot syrup, put a bandage over the sore place, and in no time he was feeling OK.

"Mom, you can't imagine how big those cobblers are," he told Sweetie. "And you can't believe how good that cobbler tasted when I licked your burned foot," she replied. "I don't think we can wait for leftovers. I say that as soon as the cobblers cool off, we help ourselves to a generous sample, tonight."

So around midnight on that first Thursday night, had you been watching, you'd have seen three of the happiest mice in all the land, gorging themselves on Pearl's homemade cherry cobbler.

After they'd taken their fill—which wasn't enough to be missed—Squeakie waxed sentimental and nostalgic.

"I was just thinking," he began, rolling a cherry pit off the table with his right front foot, "about a song they sang at the Bigtown Church which they called 'Beulah Land.' At least the older folks sang it—I don't think it ever did set too well with Reverend Doctor Moss.

"Anyway, when I'd listen to it from my hiding place in the corner down by the big pipe organ, I never dreamed we might someday live in Beulah Land. Oh, I know the sign on the highway says Tinyburg, but to me, it's Beulah Land. Let's get our pitch and see how well we do as a mouse trio. One, two, three, let's all sing:

> I've reached the land of joy divine,
> And all its riches freely mine;
> Here shines undimmed one blissful day,
> For all my night has passed away.
> O Beulah Land, sweet Beulah Land,
> As on thy highest mount I stand,
> I look away across the sea,
> Where mansions are prepared for me,
> And view the shining glory shore—
> My heav'n, my home forevermore.*

*Adapted from "Beulah Land" by Edgar Page Stites.

The Tinyburg Station

The trains don't stop at Tinyburg anymore. In fact, there aren't any trains. The quaint little station, which they call the depot, closed in 1947, soon after World War II. In the 1950s, the tracks were taken up and the railroad signals dismantled.

But the depot itself has so much charm the townspeople restored it like it was in 1895. It's saturated with nostalgia: a pot-bellied stove, signal arms, passenger benches, telegraph keys, ticket window, baggage carts, and copies of old timetables.

The Lions Club raised the money to buy and restore the station with a community bar-b-q.

The city council designated the station and grounds as a community park and museum. The one new feature they added is an old-fashioned soda fountain, complete with glass-topped tables and chairs with wire legs and backs.

The little park boasts a miniature train, picnic tables, a gazebo large enough for small musical groups, and a historical marker.

The museum is open every day during the summer. And on Saturday afternoons from May through September, the soda fountain is open and the miniature train is in operation. You can buy old-fashioned homemade ice cream on those Saturdays, or ride on the little train. It's driven by volunteers who wear striped coveralls and engineer caps, with big red handkerchiefs around their necks.

The kiddie train is free for Tinyburg youngsters. Out-of-town visitors pay only a small amount. Everyone has a great time riding or watching the train, its bell clanging and whistle blowing, while real steam pours from the smokestack.

But the major event is Old Fiddlers' Day, held each Labor

Day. Local fiddlers, banjo pickers, guitar and harmonica players fill the gazebo from early morning until dark. When the day ends, no one wants to go home.

Old-timers sitting on the benches, listening to the music, reminisce about the four passenger trains a day that once stopped at Tinyburg.

Uncle Billy Cutrell, who has the sharpest memory, says the day began when what was called the milk train pulled in at 7 AM. It picked up milk and cream from local farmers, as well as passengers.

"The mail train, due at 10:10 AM, drew the biggest crowds," Uncle Billy recalls. "A big attraction was watching the postmaster back his panel truck up to the station to unload the mail sacks. If anyone was expecting an important letter and couldn't wait for the mail to be put up at the post office, the postmaster might oblige you and sort through the sacks. Likewise, you could mail a last-minute letter on the train rather than going to the post office."

A third passenger train arrived about 4 PM, and then the last one at midnight.

The midnight train was a flag stop. The engineer braked for Tinyburg only if someone wanted to get off or on, which was unlikely. Most travelers started—or ended—their journeys long before midnight.

An exception was Mr. Jeffries, manager of the Tinyburg Variety Store. Mr. Jeffries took the midnight train once a year—in early July, when he made a buying trip to Chicago to pick out his Christmas merchandise.

"I'll always believe he left at that hour for the publicity," Uncle Billy recalls. "It was such a novelty that the *Tinyburg News* printed a brief story each July, noting that 'last Tuesday Mr. Jeffries caught the midnight train to Chicago, where he'll select the latest dolls and toys and candies for the Christmas trade.'"

One feature of Old Fiddlers' Day is an afternoon sing-along, directed by Clay Barker, president of the Tinyburg Realty Co.

Clay selects old songs about railroading, which fit the mood of the restored depot. He usually begins with:

> Early in the morning down by the station
> See, the cars are standing all in a row.
> Do you see the engineer pull the big throttle?
> Choo, choo, choo, choo, off we go!

Here's another favorite:

> I've been workin' on the railroad
> all the live-long day;
> I've been workin' on the railroad,
> just to pass the time away,
> Don't-cha hear the whistle blowin',
> rise up so early in the morn,
> Don't-cha hear the captain shoutin',
> "Dinah, blow your horn."
>
> Dinah, won't-cha blow,
> Dinah, won't-cha blow,
> Dinah, won't-cha blow your horn.
> Dinah, won't-cha blow,
> Dinah, won't-cha blow,
> Dinah won't-cha blow your horn.

Before Old Fiddlers' Day ends and the last tune's sung, you can bet someone will ask for, "She'll Be Comin' Around the Mountain."

"This is a true railroader's ballad," Uncle Billy explains each year, as if no one heard the same explanation last year. "The verse about 'breathin' smoke and fire' describes the steam engine. And the verse, 'She'll be wearin' pink pajama' is the red caboose on the end."

There must be a hundred stanzas to this old ballad, for everyone sings himself hoarse before it ends. Seven of the favorite verses begin like this:

> She'll be comin' around the mountain when she comes.
> She'll be drivin' six white horses when she comes.
> She'll be breathin' smoke and fire when she comes.

> She'll be wearin' pink pajamas when she comes.
> Oh, we'll all go out to meet her when she comes.
> We will kill the old red rooster when she comes.
> We will have chicken 'n dumplin's when she comes.

Other popular tunes include "The Rock Island Line," "The Wabash Cannon Ball," "The Chattanooga Choo-Choo," "John Henry," "The Wreck of the Old '97," "The City of New Orleans," "Night Train," and "The Blue Passenger Train."

While volunteers are cleaning up the picnic tables and taking down the Japanese lanterns, Clay Barker is likely to sing a parting solo. His strong baritone voice is heard over the neighborhood as families return to their cars or walk down the peaceful streets to their homes:

> Life is like a mountain railroad,
>   With an engineer that's brave.
> We must make the run successful
>   From the cradle to the grave;
> Watch the curves, the fills, the tunnels;
>   Never falter, never quail;
> Keep your hand upon the throttle,
>   And your eye upon the rail.
>
> You will roll up grades of trial;
>   You will cross the bridge of strife;
> See that Christ is your conductor
>   On this light'ning train of life;
> Always mindful of obstruction
>   Do your duty, never fail;
> Keep your hand upon the throttle,
>   And your eye upon the rail.
>
>   M. E. ABBEY

To visit the Tinyburg depot with its original furnishings, follow the highway seven miles out of Pretense. At the edge of town, you'll recognize this big billboard which the residents painted and erected themselves:

> Welcome to Tinyburg: the only city in the United States with an unlisted zip code.

The best time to visit the depot is on Labor Day, when you can hear the fiddlers.

While you're there, walk over to a grassy plot just east of the depot. There, inside a protective iron fence, is a marker:

Tinyburg Depot
1895-1947
"Those were the days!"

Also engraved on the marker is a brief essay, written by a railroad conductor who says he called out, "Tinyburg— Tinyburg—next stop!" so many times he still says it in his sleep. For a copy of the essay, you can ask for one inside the depot. Copies are free, and they make nice souvenirs:

The Station
by Robert J. Hastings

Tucked away in our subconscious minds is a vision—an idyllic vision— in which we see ourselves on a long journey that spans an entire continent. We're traveling by train and, from the windows, we drink in the passing scenes of cars on nearby highways, of children waving at crossings, of cattle grazing in distant pastures, of smoke pouring from power plants, of row upon row of cotton and corn and wheat, of flatlands and valleys, of city skylines and village halls.

But uppermost in our conscious minds is our final destination—for at a certain hour and on a given day, our train will pull into the station with bells ringing, flags waving, and bands playing. And once that day comes, so many wonderful dreams will come true, and all the jagged pieces of our lives will fit together like a completed jigsaw puzzle. So, restlessly, we pace the aisles and count the miles, peering ahead, cursing the minutes for loitering, waiting, waiting, waiting for the station. . . .

"Yes, when we reach the station, that will be it," we cry. "When we're eighteen! When we buy that new 450 SL Mercedes Benz! When we put the last kid through college! When we win that promotion! When we pay off the mortgage! When we retire!" Yes, from that day on, like the heroes and heroines of a child's fairy tale, we will all live happily ever after.

Sooner or later, however, we must realize there is no station, no one place to arrive at once and for all. The journey is the joy. The station is an illusion—it constantly outdistances us. Yesterday's a memory; tomorrow's a dream. Yesterday belongs to history; tomorrow belongs to God. Yesterday's a fading sunset; tomorrow's a faint sunrise. So gently close the door on yesterday and throw the key away, for only today is there light enough to live and love. It isn't the burden's of today that drive men mad. Rather, it's regret over yesterday and fear of tomorrow. Regret and fear are the twin thieves who would rob us of that Golden Treasure we call today, this tiny strip of light between two nights.

"Relish the moment" is a good motto, especially when coupled with Psalm 118:24, "This is the day which the Lord hath made; we will rejoice and be glad in it."

So stop pacing the aisles and counting the miles. Instead, swim more rivers, climb more mountains, kiss more babies, count more stars. Laugh more and cry less. Go barefoot oftener. Eat more ice cream. Ride more merry-go-rounds. Watch more sunsets. Life must be lived as we go along. The station will come soon enough.

Tinyburg's Zip Code

The part-time secretary at the Tinyburg Church was ready to order new stationery when the printing salesman suggested she wait a few days. "The government's issuing a zip code for every post office in the country," he advised. "After that, all mail will require a zip code, regardless of where its sent. Tinyburg will have its own zip code too, which should be printed on your new stationery."

"You mean Tinyburg's getting a number of its very own?" she asked, incredulously. "At least one," the salesman explained. "Larger cities such as Bigtown will be assigned several zip codes, broken down into neighborhoods. This will make it easier to sort and deliver the mail."

"I wonder what Tinyburg's number will be?" the secretary thought out loud. The salesman replied that no one knew at this point, not even the postmaster. "We'll just have to wait," he said.

The postmaster at Tinyburg felt a little uneasy when the first listings of the new zip codes arrived, but he kept it to himself. You see, the first lists, which were for his own county, omitted Tinyburg. And when the state list came and then the regional list, well, Tinyburg was nowhere to be found.

Certain it was an oversight, the postmaster made no complaint with the postal service in Washington.

"When in the world are we going to get our zip code?" the church secretary asked the postmaster a few days later when she stopped in to buy some stamps. "Be patient," the postmaster replied. "We'll get our number in time. The government has a foolproof method for assigning the numbers through its computer system. There's no way Tinyburg could be overlooked."

The weeks dragged by. No Tinyburg zip code ever appeared in any of the revised lists which came from Washington. The church stationery ran out.

The secretary thought it important enough to raise the issue at the next church business meeting. "Folks, I need some guidelines," she announced. "There's not a sheet of stationery in the church building, and I don't want the blame for typing letters on mimeograph paper. Are we getting a zip code, or aren't we? Shall I reorder stationery like we had, with no zip code? I'd hate to think every church in the whole United States except Tinyburg had a zip code on its stationery. That could put us in a bad light and make us look backward and countrified."

The postmaster, who was a member of the church, promised to call the postal service in Washington the very next morning to learn, once and for all, what was going on. The report he received was not too encouraging.

"Mr. Postmaster," the official in Washington answered, "all zip codes were assigned months ago by our master computer. You should have been the first to be notified of Tinyburg's number. There's an oversight somewhere. I'll investigate and put a letter in the mail this afternoon confirming your number. There has to be a number for you somewhere."

The letter arrived on Saturday morning. Knowing the keen interest of many of the church folks, the postmaster asked permission to read it to the congregation on Sunday morning.

Citizens of Tinyburg: We have made a thorough investigation which shows, for some unknown reason, that the master computer failed to assign Tinyburg a zip code. Since all the codes have been compiled and published by states and counties, it is not practical at this time to assign you a number. Were we to do so, it would confuse the numbering system and cause no end of confusion.

We think, however, that we have arrived at a solution which will make everyone happy. Bigtown, which isn't far from Tinyburg, was assigned a total of seven zip codes. Since one of the rural routes from Bigtown extends almost to Tinyburg, we have decided to lengthen that route to include Tinyburg. That route, which is number eight, has its own zip code, which is the one you are to use on your mail.

This means that starting January 1, all mail to Tinyburg should be addressed Rural Route 8, Bigtown, followed by the appropriate zip code. Admittedly, this will delay your mail a few hours each day since the rural carrier can't drop yours off until he completes his route.

We regret to inform you that this will also eliminate the need for a Tinyburg post office. Your office will be closed effective January 1. Please notify your patrons that after such date, they will purchase their stamps and mail their packages at the post office in Bigtown.

Never has a letter that had so little to do with the internal affairs of the Tinyburg Church caused so much concern.

Clay Barker, president of the Tinyburg Realty Company, was on his feet immediately, his face flushed and beads of perspiration forming on his forehead.

"Mr. Postmaster," Clay began. "That letter you just read promises to make everyone happy. It does just the opposite. It makes everyone unhappy. And it makes me very unhappy. I don't know anyone who's pleased. Computer or no computer, we're not taking a back seat to Bigtown. I'll have the whole world to know that the Tinyburg Realty Company is in Tinyburg, not at the end of Rural Route 8 of Bigtown. In fact, my firm's not at the end of anything, and the same goes for our church and our homes and everyone and everybody here."

"Gentlemen, gentlemen," interrupted the Preacher. "Let me remind you this is merely announcement time during a public worship service. This is not a town meeting. I know our concern. But this isn't the place for such a discussion. Besides, other residents who are not here will want a say-so."

"That's part of the problem," shot back Clay. "No one's had a say-so in any of this. Some computer way off in Washington bumped us off the face of the earth—or tried to. No warm-blooded human being would do that to a town as nice as Tinyburg, and I'm here to say that for one, I'm not going to take it sitting down.

"And, yes, I do think it's a church matter, for it's a moral matter. We've gone number crazy, a code for this and a code for that. Anytime our government takes a high-handed notion toward its citizens, makes them feel like nobodies, I call that negative morality."

The Preacher could tell by the shuffling of feet, the whispering comments, and looks of apprehension on the faces of the worshipers that it was useless to proceed with the regular order of service.

"Granted this isn't a town meeting, and that we're not a government agency, and that we can't speak for the whole community, I'll delay my sermon 'till everyone has his say," announced the Preacher. "Who wants to speak next?"

"I do," announced Aunt Sarah Biggs, one of the leading Bible scholars in the church. "Frankly, I disapprove of the entire zip code system. All these years, we've never needed a number to tell us who we are and where we get our mail. Tinyburg's in Tinyburg, and Bigtown's in Bigtown. Everyone knows that. Now the Bible speaks of the mark of the beast, of numbers in people's foreheads. Maybe this is a sign of the last days, giving everybody a number for everything.

"Now just stop and count all the numbers floating around. Take me, for example. I have a house number and a Social Security number. And I have my number for a driver's license; and another one for my car license plate. And my phone number, plus an area code. And a number for my Sears credit card and another for my bank account. Who needs more numbers? If so take some of mine! So I make a motion we petition the officials in Washington to nullify the whole zip code conspiracy and let Tinyburg be Tinyburg and Bigtown be Bigtown."

"I know you mean well, Aunt Sarah," reminded the Preacher, "but this isn't a church conference. Besides, it's out of order for us to speak for all of Tinyburg on a matter that's out of our hands, anyway."

William J. Cutrell, whose nickname is Uncle Billy-Told-You-So, was the next on his feet. Clearing his throat, Uncle Billy began, "I"ve been sitting here thinking about my situation. Not everyone can afford to do what I've decided, but I intend to boycott the entire United States mail system. I can get along without the mail, thank you.

"First thing tomorrow morning, I'm taking down my mailbox and notifying the post office to return everything that's addressed to me. My Social Security check goes to the bank, anyway, so I can live without mail, zip or no zip. Nor will I mail anything to anyone. I can use the telephone for what little communicating I do. 'Course, I'm just one out of millions, and what I decide won't matter, but it makes me feel good. I'll accept no mail addressed to William J. Cutrell at Route 8, Bigtown, and that's that. If we're not good enough for a zip code, then the whole postal system isn't good enough for me, period."

"Uncle Billy, that may be OK for you," replied Clay Barker. "But business folks like me depend on the mail. We've got to find a better solution. And I know just the fellow who can advise us. He's sitting up there on the third row—Burt David, a securities salesman who retired here from Bigtown. He's lived in big cities, knows how to get action. What about it, Burt?"

It was apparent that Burt was pleased as he stood to give his opinion.

"Friends," he began, "it's true we're just a handful. But if we holler loud enough, someone will listen. We've got to put our fingers on the nerve center of government. So let's start calling. Forget the mail and do like Uncle Billy—use the telephone. Call anyone and everyone. Call, the police. Call the mayor. Call the dogcatcher. Call the governor. Call your state representatives. Call your congressmen. Call your senators. Call the

secretary of state. Call the FBI. Call the attorney-general. Call
the president. Call his cabinet. Call the Supreme Court. Call
the president of General Motors. Call the *New York Times*.
Call, call, call is my advice. I've seen it work before."

"Amen! Amen! Amen!" shouted the congregation. "That's
telling 'em! Go to it! Speak up! Carry on! Get us a zip code!"

And carry on they did. Rarely has a community so small
been heard so clearly. Suddenly, everyone in the country knew
about Tinyburg. It became a household word. Paul Harvey
picked up the issue on his noon broadcast. CBS evening news
sent a camera crew to interview the Tinyburg postmaster and
Clay Barker. *Newsweek* magazine called Aunt Sarah and Uncle Billy for their comments. *Time* magazine published a
photo of the Tinyburg post office with the caption, "The town
that Washington forgot."

The result was what Burt David predicted: government officials were suddenly chagrined that in this day of so-called
faultless computers, one of the most progressive communities
in the nation had been completely overlooked.

Finally, a compromise was reached. A second letter arrived
from Washington. The *Tinyburg News* published it in its en-
tirety:

> Citizens of Tinyburg: First, our apologies to each of you.
> No one intended to ignore your fine community. Nor, on sec-
> ond thought, do we feel it fair to assign you one of Bigtown's
> zip codes. On the other hand, confusion would result if we
> should assign and list a number for you in the national direc-
> tory. So we propose to give you an unlisted number.
>
> We pledge your mail will be delivered, zip code or no zip
> code. Every postal employee has been so informed. If you
> wish to share the number with your correspondents, do so.
> However, please do not publish it or print it on stationery or
> the like. Yours is the only community in the nation with an
> unlisted zip code. Also, this new policy allows your post office
> to remain open.

Since the folks in Tinyburg need little excuse for a party, the
Lions Club quickly announced a city-wide barbecue to cele-

brate the good news. There the postmaster cautioned everyone about putting the new number in print, urging them instead to memorize it. That night, many parents drilled their preschoolers until they could recite the number also.

The following Sunday, the Preacher spoke on "God's Numbering System." Some wondered if he was about to reveal some secret key to Tinyburg's new zip code, maybe buried for centuries in the numerology of the Old Testament or in Revelation. But he had no such grandiose ambitions. Here's a summary of what he did say:

> According to Psalm 147:4, "He telleth the number of the stars; he calleth them all by their names." And Matthew 10:30 says, "But the very hairs of your head are all numbered." These verses describe our Lord's marvelous numbering system. As we look into the vast universe, we are reminded that God has inventoried every star. His marvelous wisdom counts them all, apart from computer or calculator. Not a single star, buried in the farthest recesses of space, is unknown to Him.
>
> As we look closer, right here in Tinyburg, we are reminded that our heavenly Father knows us so well that every hair of our heads is numbered. Oh, I don't mean He keeps a daily count, although He could if He chose. What this means is that nothing's too small to be overlooked by our Father. You and I, being human, make mistakes in adding and subtracting. Our officials in Washington made an honest mistake. But we must forgive.
>
> So long as we have faith in a God who knows His creation, we needn't fret about man-made license numbers, phone numbers, and even zip codes. In closing, let me quote another verse from the tenth chapter of Matthew: "Are not two sparrows sold for a farthing? and one of them shall not fall on the ground without your Father." Wherever you live, whatever you need, however you hurt, God knows. We're His children, not numbers in a computer.

To close the service, the Preacher asked Candice Spiller to sing "His Eye Is on the Sparrow."

And as the folks were dismissed and mingled in the churchyard, the sophisticated number system of a computerized world seemed strange and far away. For a few moments, at least, they were persons again.

If you'd like to visit Tinyburg, the directions are simple. It's just seven miles south of Pretense. As you approach this little village of 1,473 residents, you'll spot a huge billboard:

> Welcome to Tinyburg—The only city in the US with an unlisted zip code!

Yes, they insist on calling themselves a city. And should you ever get a letter from the Tinyburg Church, don't look for a zip code on their new stationery. It's quite a status symbol around town to know the zip code, so don't expect anyone to tell you what it is. Oh, Uncle Billy did slip and tell me, but on the condition that I wouldn't tell you!

Clay Runs for President

One of the best things that ever happened to Jimmie Swan was the day the state rehabilitation department helped get him a job as a dishwasher at the Tinyburg Nursing Home.

Although Jimmie is a slow learner as far as book learning, he's a genius in two respects: keeping the kitchen spotless and making friends.

Although it may be 10:30 AM by the time Jimmie finishes the breakfast dishes, they sparkle and shine as if they'd just come out of a department showroom. And the residents love him. Although there's a big gap in their ages, Jimmie knows each one by his first name. And he's always doing something extra that he's not paid for—such as fluffing a pillow, mailing a letter, finding a misplaced pair of glasses, walking a patient in the morning sunshine, or hugging an old man who's just learned his best friend died last night.

There are two services at the Tinyburg Church which Jimmie never misses. These are morning worship on Sundays and the monthly church conference or business meeting.

Although invariably late on Sunday mornings, Jimmie will sit nowhere but the center of the middle pew, three rows from the front. "I like to look right at the Preacher" is how Jimmie explains his preference for the middle section.

Members have long since learned to leave space for him, for regardless of how crowded the sanctuary, Jimmie will climb over anyone or anything to reach his favorite seat. Visitors sometimes get upset when asked to scoot over and make room. But once Jimmie flashes his famous smile, they overlook the inconvenience (or ignore the pain of a toe he just stepped on!).

"Preacher, looks like I'm always late," Jimmie apologized

one Sunday after services. "But the cooks serve hot cakes and sausage on Sunday morning,, and you know how hard it is to clean the dishes of all that syrup."

One Sunday Jimmie arrived just as the Preacher was saying the benediction: "The Lord be gracious to you, and give you peace. Amen."

"The dishwasher broke down and I had to do all the dishes by hand," Jimmie told Uncle Billy afterwards as they stood out on the church lawn.

For the monthly church conference, Jimmie cares little about where he sits so long as it's next to Clay Barker. One reason he prefers to sit next to Clay is that Clay gives him tips on how to vote. Jimmie usually whispers, "Mr. Barker, I don't understand the motion: how should I vote?" Some members say this isn't fair, for it means Clay gets two votes on every proposal! But no one's ever made an issue of it, for they know Jimmie means well.

Oh, Jimmie's habit did cause a little stir one night. Members were trying to decide on whether to leave the clock on a side wall where it had been for years or to relocate it at the back. "Leave it where's it's always been," some argued. "That way everyone knows what time it is." The other side argued, "Move it to the back so only the Preacher can see it. Folks should keep theirs minds on the sermon—not what time it is."

Tension mounted to where someone called for a secret ballot. So the moderator announced, "If you want the clock moved to the back of the auditorium, vote yes. If you wish the clock to stay where it's been for as long as some can remember, vote no."

As ballots and pencils were distributed, Jimmie grew nervous. How would he know which to vote? Oh, he understood that the issue was over the location of the clock. But more important to him was voting the way Clay voted, so great was his confidence in Clay. Actually, it mattered little to Jimmie where the clock was placed.

Since it was a secret ballot, Jimmie knew it wasn't proper to ask Clay. So he got a bright idea. He wrote on his ballot, "I vote like Mr. Barker."

The tellers smiled when they opened Jimmie's ballot, knowing it couldn't be counted either way, for no one knew how Clay had voted.

But their smiles turned to puzzled looks when they discovered it was a tie vote, not counting Jimmie's ballot. This meant that if Jimmie voted one way or another, he would break the tie. Not wishing to embarrass him, one of the tellers went back into the auditorium, sat down beside Jimmie, and explained the problem. Jimmie nodded, asked for a new ballot, and immediately wrote, "I vote to take the clock out of the church altogether." He spoke the words aloud as he wrote.

Somehow this broke the tension, and everyone started laughing, good-naturedly. When things quieted down, Uncle Billy Cutrell took the floor. "Folks," he began, "this may not be procedurally correct, but I move that, since Jimmie was to cast the deciding vote, we make his vote just that—a decision to take the clock out of the church altogether, maybe put it out in the vestibule." Then, with a sly, "I told-you-so look," Uncle Billy added, "if you ask me, the Preacher needs a calendar lots worse than a clock, anyway. At times, I think it's Monday by the time he reaches the benediction!"

And so, believe it or not, that's what everyone agreed on. The evening ended well, and as folks made their way home, they agreed that the world's living too fast anyway, and maybe it's good to find a quiet place to worship free from the restless minute hands of a man-made clock. Old-timers around the church still refer to that night as "Jimmie's business meeting."

Of course, that story can hardly hold a candle to what happened at another conference when members were electing a church moderator. The person holding this office presides at each business session and serves as an ex officio member on all committees. Since the job carries a lot of prestige, Clay Barker announced to his wife one year that he was thinking about running for election.

"Clay, in a church you don't run for office, like politicians," she scolded. "Whoever heard of a member putting himself up for election? If someone chooses to nominate you, fine. But, please don't embarrass your family by announcing your so-called candidacy."

"You don't understand," Clay answered. "Ever since S. Franklin Rodd beat me for county tax assessor, I've wanted to run for something, to show I've got friends, too. After all the years and money and sacrifice I've put in that church, surely I'm not unreasonable in wanting to be moderator."

However, Clay yielded to his wife's advice, mentioning his dream only to Jimmie Swan, and that in a casual way.

When the big night came, several persons were nominated as moderator but not Clay. Jimmie, seated next to him, noted how Clay dropped his head, his chin resting on his chest, when the nominations were closed. Jimmie put his arm around Clay's shoulders, giving him a quick, reassuring hug.

After the voting ended, and time came to adjourn, Jimmie did something he'd never braved before. He stood to his feet and made a motion.

"I nominate Clay Barker for president of the United States," he beamed.

At first, there was a long, awkward pause. Then two or three snickers were heard. Was this a joke? Was Jimmie trying to embarrass Clay? The look on Jimmie's face said that he was dead serious.

Then the Preacher explained, "Jimmie, this isn't the place to make nominations for our country's president. That's done by political parties. Besides, it isn't even the year for a presidential election."

"I don't care what year it is," Jimmie replied, "Clay Barker's fit to be president of the whole United States. This is a free country. We're a delib . . . a deliverrative body. I can nominate him if I want to."

Mrs. Barker broke the tension by saying how nice it would be to move into the White House as the president's wife. "But Jimmie, Clay doesn't have time to go Washington, even if elected. His work's piled up so he can't even replace my clothesline posts that fell over in last winter's ice storm!"

"But I like Mr. Barker," Jimmie replied. "He has lots more ability than folks in Tinyburg think. He could run the whole country. And besides, he knows how to be nice to people. Ain't that worth somethin'?"

Someone called for the benediction, and the meeting closed without further comment. Aunt Sarah Biggs, who as clerk of the conference was keeping the minutes, asked if she should make a record of Jimmie's motion, but no one seemed to want to answer her.

The next Sunday morning, Clay Barker invited himself to breakfast at the Tinyburg Nursing Home. "When I learned you folks have hot cakes every Sunday morning, I couldn't resist," he told one of the residents across the table from him.

After breakfast, Clay busied himself, clearing the tables and helping Jimmie scrape the dishes for the dishwasher. "That pancake syrup sure sticks to the plates," he commented to Jimmie. "No wonder you're late for services every Sunday!"

But that morning, worshipers were surprised to see Jimmie and Clay arrive on time. Jimmie upset no one in finding his favorite pew.

During the organ prelude, Jimmie whispered to Clay, "Mr. Barker, I still think you'd make a swell president. You're good at everything . . . and nice to everybody. That's what it takes to be head of somethin'.

Clay squeezed Jimmie's knee, then replied, "Jimmie, there's only one thing better than being president. That's knowing you think I ought to be."

Just before the Preacher's sermon, the children's choir sang "Brighten the Corner Where You Are!"

"That's me," Clay said to himself. "Brightening my little corner right here in Tinyburg. Guess that's big enough job for any man my age."

I hope you'll visit Tinyburg sometime. It's easy to find—just seven miles south of Pretense. You're practically there when you see the big billboard:

> Welcome to Tinyburg: The only city in the United States with an unlisted zip code

Tinyburg's a place where the air's clean and pure, and everyone sleeps well at night just like the Sominex ads promise. It's a town where all the children say, "Yes, ma'am," and "No, ma'am," and "Yes, sir," and "No, sir." And if residents stop and ask how you're feeling, they'll likely take time to listen to what you say.

Oh, one other thing. If you go on a Sunday, don't sit on the third row. That's Jimmie's pew, and he never fails to show up—even if he's just in time for the benediction!

An Autumn Tree

Ordinarily Uncle Billy Cutrell is loyal to his Preacher. He listens attentively to his sermons, votes for most of his proposals, and puts in a good word whenever some loafer at the Tinyburg Cafe jokes about his faults.

But one fall when the Preacher announced a new sermon series on the trees of the Bible, he arched his eyebrows as if they were question marks:

"What in the world do trees have to do with the gospel? We need more preaching on sin and old-fashioned godliness, not lessons in botany."

But he sat patiently through the series, figuring the Preacher knew what he was doing.

The Preacher based his first sermon on Genesis 2:17, "But of the tree of the knowledge of good and evil, thou shalt not eat of it." This passage dealt with the temptation of Adam and Eve in the Garden of Eden, and how God set aside one tree whose fruit they were forbidden to eat.

The Preacher's second message, "The Palm-Tree Christian," dealt with two verses in the Psalms. The first was Psalm 1:3, "And he shall be like a tree planted by the rivers of water, that bringeth forth his fruit in his season." The other was Psalm 92:12, "The righteous shall flourish like the palm tree." He went into great detail describing the root system of palm trees in the desert, how they reach deep into the soil for moisture. He pleaded for Christians to guard against shallow living.

For his third sermon, the Preacher selected Matthew 3:10 as a text, "Every tree which bringeth not forth good fruit is hewn down, and cast into the fire." He emphasized that Christians who bear no fruit are as worthless as a peach tree that never grows a peach.

By the time the Preacher reached his fourth sermon on trees, Uncle Billy decided he'd heard all he wanted to hear about trees, but he listened respectfully. The topic was the crucifixion, based on 1 Peter 2:24, "Who his own self bare our sins in his own body on the tree."

The last sermon about trees was on heaven, the text Revelation 22:2, "In the midst of the street of it [heaven] . . . was there the tree of life . . . and the leaves of the tree were for the healing of the nations."

Monday morning after tree sermon number five, Uncle Billy was raking leaves when Aunt Sarah Biggs passed on her way to a Bible class at the Tinyburg Nursing Home.

"Good morning, Aunt Sarah," nodded Uncle Billy. "Don't guess you're going to talk to the old folks this morning about trees?" he asked, good-naturedly.

"I sure could if I wanted to," she replied quickly. "Do you realize the Good Book mentions trees over two hundred times?"

Uncle Billy knew not to question anything Aunt Sarah said about the Bible. Even the Preacher said that so long as he can reach Aunt Sarah by phone, he has little need for a Bible concordance: "That woman can tell you chapter and verse for nearly any passage you want to find, quicker than you can say John the Baptist."

"Since you raised the subject of trees and I'm early for my class at the nursing home, I'll rest a minute on your front steps and enlighten you on trees of the Bible," Aunt Sarah continued, with a mischievous glint in her eyes.

"Sorry I raised the subject," Uncle Billy said under his breath, but too low for Aunt Sarah to hear.

"Uncle Billy, I'll bet you a gold star on your attendance

record at Sunday School that you can't tell me how many varieties of trees are mentioned in the Bible?"

"Never figured it was that important," Uncle Billy replied, leaning on his rake handle, the bright yellow and red leaves falling gently on his oversize, straw cowboy hat.

"Listen to me, Uncle Billy, anything the good Lord put in his Book's important. He had a reason for every word and comma and period and question mark. Now to answer my own question, the Bible mentions at least eighteen varieties of trees.

"Let's see . . . the almond, apple, bay, box, cedar, chestnut, shittah, fig, juniper, fir, mulberry, and myrtle. And oh yes, there's the olive, palm, pine, pomegranate, sycamore, and willow—all eighteen of them!"

Uncle Billy admitted the list was fascinating, but he staged a mock yawn as if it didn't matter to him if there were a *hundred* and eighteen trees in the Bible."

"Well and good. But that's no excuse for our Preacher taking up five Sundays with trees. When I go to church, I want preaching, not a botany lesson."

"He wasn't giving botany lessons," Aunt Sarah replied impatiently, as if she were addressing a four-year-old. "Ministers often choose examples from everyday life, sort of an object lesson or parable, to illustrate gospel truths. And what's more common, yet more beautiful and beneficial, than trees?"

"Just look at these beautiful colors, as if God took a giant set of watercolors and brushed the leaves with every hue imaginable. And trees furnish lumber for homes and furniture. And fruits for apple and peach pies, and hickory nuts for homemade fudge, and pecans for. . . ."

"Stop, stop!" interrupted Uncle Billy. "My stomach's already growling for a midmorning snack, and here you're tantalizing me with pecan pie, my favorite."

"That's one problem with menfolk," she replied. "Mind's always on their stomach."

Then seriously, "Another thing, Uncle Billy, think how much we owe those neighbors who set out these trees here on your street. Most of them are gone now, but the trees keep on growing, shading us in summer, thrilling us each fall with their brilliant colors. And that's the point the Preacher was making—this old world needs strength and stability, something we know will be here tomorrow when we wake up and face a new day. And Christians can be like them, trustworthy, their roots deep in their faith, their faces bright like the first leaves of spring."

With that, Aunt Sarah picked up her big black Bible and continued down the street to the nursing home. And Uncle Billy went back to raking leaves into big, fluffy piles.

That afternoon, he walked over to the Tinyburg Florist and bought a little pin oak seedling. "Lightning killed one of my big oaks near the street several summers ago," he told the sales clerk, "and I never did get around to replacing it. 'Course I won't be around to rake many of its leaves, but these little tykes running up and down the sidewalks, playing hop-scotch and riding their tricycles, maybe they will."

It was late afternoon when Aunt Sarah passed Uncle Billy's on her way home. He was so busy tamping the soil around the seedling that he never looked up. That night, Aunt Sarah, who's also an amateur poet, wrote these lines in her journal:

> I saw a man planting a tree,
>   an old man.
> And it was November, the sky
>   grey as in dying.
> And the man was in the November
>   of his life.
> But buried in the tree—its limbs
>   and roots—
> Were buds and leaves and green
>   and gold and brown.

And shade for pilgrims weary.
And branches sturdy for climbing.
 for youngsters bent on scaling,
 for pirates climbing masts.
I saw a man planting a tree,
 an old man.
And it was November.

CHRISTIAN HERALD
People Making a Difference

Christian Herald is a family of dedicated, Christ-centered ministries that reaches out to deprived children in need, and to homeless men who are lost in alcoholism and drug addiction. Christian Herald also offers the finest in family and evangelical literature through its book club and publishes a popular, dynamic magazine for today's Christians.

Our Ministries

Christian Herald Children. The door of God's grace opens wide to give impoverished youngsters a breath of fresh air, away from the evils of the streets. Every summer, hundreds of youngsters are welcomed at the Christian Herald Mont Lawn Camp located in the Poconos at Bushkill, Pennsylvania. Year-round assistance is also provided, including teen programs, tutoring in reading and writing, family counseling, career guidance and college scholarship programs.

The Bowery Mission. Located in New York City, the Bowery Mission offers hope and Gospel strength to the downtrodden and homeless. Here, the men of Skid Row are fed, clothed, ministered to. Many voluntarily enter a 6-month discipleship program of spiritual guidance, nutrition therapy and Bible study.

Our Father's House. Our Father's House is a discipleship program located in a rural setting in Lancaster County, Pennsylvania, which enables addicts to take the last steps on the road to a useful Christian life.

Paradise Lake Retreat Center. During the spring, fall and winter months, our children's camp at Bushkill, Pennsylvania, becomes a lovely retreat for religious gatherings of up to 200. Excellent accommodations include an on-site chapel, heated cabins, large meeting areas, recreational facilities, and delicious country-style meals. Write to: Paradise Lake Retreat Center, Box 252, Bushkill, PA 18234, or call: (717) 588-6067.

Christian Herald Magazine is contemporary—a dynamic publication that addresses the vital concerns of today's Christian. Each issue contains a sharing of true personal stories written by people who have found in Christ the strength to make a difference in the world around them.

Family Bookshelf provides a wide selection of wholesome, inspirational reading and Christian literature written by best-selling authors. All books are recommended by an Advisory Board of distinguished writers and editors.

* * *

Christian Herald ministries, founded in 1878, are supported by the voluntary contributions of individuals and by legacies and bequests. Contributions are tax deductible. Checks should be made out to: Christian Herald Children, Bowery Mission, or Christian Herald Association.

Fully-accredited Member
of the Evangelical Council
for Financial Accountability

Administrative Office:
40 Overlook Drive
Chappaqua, New York 10514
Telephone: (914) 769-9000